BANEFORD BOOK 3

A MEMORY OF TOMORROW

ALI KADEN

A MEMORY OF TOMORROW
BANEFORD BOOK 3

Copyright © 2024 By Ali Kaden. All rights reserved.

Edited by: George Verongos

ISBN: 9798328700580

VISIT ALI KADEN'S WEBSITE FOR THE LATEST UPDATES:
WWW.ALIKADENBOOKS.COM

AUTHOR'S NOTE

There is no town named Baneford in Massachusetts. Its history, landmarks, and residents are fictional. All other characters in the book are also fictional, although some places mentioned are real.

CONTENTS

CHAPTER 1 1

CHAPTER 2 7

CHAPTER 3 19

CHAPTER 4 31

CHAPTER 5 43

CHAPTER 6 53

CHAPTER 7 69

CHAPTER 8 81

CHAPTER 9 91

CHAPTER 10 101

CHAPTER 11 115

CHAPTER 12 125

CHAPTER 13 137

CHAPTER 14 153

ABOUT THE AUTHOR 157

CHAPTER 1

THE SUN DIPPED below the horizon, casting the sky in a dramatic palette of burnt orange and deep purple. This twilight canopy hung over a serene landscape punctuated by rolling green hills and ancient trees. Nestled among these natural monuments, a series of stone enclosures rose from the earth. These structures were composed of large, interconnected circular formations, each defined by massive limestone pillars towering above the terrain, their surfaces intricately carved with bas-reliefs. The carvings depicted a diverse mix of animals—foxes in mid-hunt, lions stalking prey, and birds in flight, revealing a deep connection to the natural world. As dusk deepened, the shadows of the pillars stretched out over the land, casting long, dark fingers across the earth, as if reaching into the present from a distant, mystical past.

At the entrance of the largest enclosure, about a dozen men and women stood firm, ready to defend their ancestral grounds. They were adorned in garments fashioned from animal hides and roughly spun wool, which hung in tatters from their worn and rugged frames. Each warrior bore distinctive war paint streaked across their faces—bold lines of black and red, symbols of their vows to protect their home.

In their hands, they clutched an array of primitive weapons, spears tipped with sharpened stone, sturdy bows strung tight with sinew, and clubs studded with bits of flint. Their knuckles turned white, every muscle tensed and ready for the battle that loomed. They were the last defenders of sacred ground. As the chill of the evening settled around them, the rustle of leaves and occasional snap of a twig underfoot were the only sounds that pierced the silence.

Behind the determined ranks of defenders, a man and a woman stood together, preparing for an ancient ritual. Outlined against the dusky sky, the man with broad shoulders radiated a quiet strength. Beside him, the woman moved with fluidity. Their dark, flowing hair whipped about them in the breeze, and their bronzed skin glowed under the fading light. Together, they knelt in the coarse sand at the heart of the largest stone circle. They began to trace a complex array of symbols—intricate characters made up of circles and lines that intertwined like the roots of a tree.

As they completed the circle of symbols, they slowly rose to their feet, their eyes meeting in a silent exchange that spoke of shared years and a deep understanding—the intimacy of husband and wife. Then, turning their palms upward towards the sky, they began to chant. Their voices, harmoniously intertwined, rose rhythmically, carried by the wind, reaching upward to the stars, calling for protection and power in the face of evil.

The quiet was broken by a deep rumble. Over the top of the nearest hill, four giants appeared, towering and monstrous, like deformed versions of men. They stood as tall as the ancient temples dotting the landscape. Each giant looked roughly human, but exaggerated and misshapen. Their skin was thick and rough, marked by scars and pockmarks from numerous battles. Their beards were bushy and their hair, long and tangled, was tied into thick braids. Deep-set eyes gave them a predatory look as they scanned the horizon.

Two of the giants wielded enormous broadswords, gleaming dully in the fading light. As they moved, vibrations could be felt even at a distance. Their roars, deep and guttural, sliced through the air, echoing off the stone structures. As they came down the hill towards the stone enclosure, a wave of panic swept through the assembled defenders.

A young warrior, his eyes wide with both fear and determination, charged forward to confront the approaching giants. Clutching his spear tightly, he let out a determined yell and threw it with all his strength. The spear flew straight, sinking deep into the thigh of the nearest behemoth. The massive creature roared in rage but continued to advance.

In the brief moment of stunned silence, the other tribespeople reacted instinctively. One woman, darted to the left, using the cover of the large stone pillars to shield herself. Another man went right flank, moving stealthily along the perimeter of the enclosure, knife in hand.

As the giants neared the entrance of the enclosure, the one who had been speared acted swiftly. He reached down and seized the warrior who had struck him. Before anyone could intervene, the goliath hoisted the man high above his head and then brutally tore him in two. The warrior's remains spilled to the ground in a bloody heap.

A gasp of horror rose from the tribe, and from the man and woman performing the incantations in the back of the main enclosure. Fueled by a mix of rage and despair, others charged, only to be met with overwhelming force. Giant fists crashed down, and the sweep of gargantuan swords cleaved through the air, ending lives in sprays of blood and cries of anguish. Four more defenders fell, their bodies broken on the trampled earth.

The remaining defenders quickly formed a shield wall at the entrance, trying to protect the couple still chanting inside. The giant marked with concentric circles on his chest moved forward, his huge sword wet with the blood of those he had slain. He broke through the defenders easily, killing as he went, and then halted to look at the man and woman. As he stared, they stopped chanting, and a sudden flash lit up the sky. They looked up to see the three belt stars of Orion pulsating brightly, shining like a beacon above them.

The couple quickly knelt and picked up flint stones, their hands trembling as they struck them together. Sparks flew and ignited the brush soaked in cedar sap, creating a trail of fire leading to the enclosure's entrance where the giant stood. Flames burst forth, swift and voracious.

Caught in the flames, the giant bellowed in agony. His massive form writhed as the fire consumed him, his cries of pain echoing into the night. Over the roar of the fire, the man shouted.

"Run, now!" He grabbed the woman's hand, and together they rushed to the rear wall of the enclosure.

They climbed quickly, grabbing at the rough stone edges that jutted out from the wall. When they reached the top of the fourteen-foot barrier, they sat briefly on the wide ledge, catching their breath. Turning around, they saw the giant rising from the flames. His body was charred, smoke rising off him, but he was still coming, his eyes burning with anger. The sight spurred them into action.

Jumping off the ledge, they landed on the grassy hillside below, and immediately ran towards the dense woods. The giant's roars of anger echoed behind them, growing fainter as they disappeared into the dark trees. Behind them, smoke from their homeland curled into the night sky.

***

Adrian awoke with a gasp, his body sweaty, heart racing as if he were still running through those ancient woods. The memory of the dream clung to him with unsettling clarity—flames, giants, and the desperate escape over the enclosure. Beside him, Evelyn lay sleeping peacefully, her breathing steady and calm.

The room was dim, lit only by the first hints of dawn peering through the curtains. Adrian lay there, trying to steady his breathing, trying to make sense of the vivid nightmare that felt more like a memory. Something ancient and forgotten was stirring within him, a tale of a past life that refused to remain silent.

Evelyn stirred, then sighed. Adrian watched her for a moment, pushing down his desire to share the memory of his dream with her.

"Another dream?" she whispered; her voice still hoarse with sleep.

"Yes," he nodded.

"Tell me."

Adrian turned to face her, his eyes reflecting more sadness than she expected to see.

"I was in this vast, green landscape," he began, his voice low. "There were these enormous stone structures. Then there were giants, terrifying and brutal. They stormed through this enclosure."

Evelyn's hand tightened around his. She could see the intensity in his eyes.

"The giants were unstoppable," Adrian continued, his voice catching slightly. "There was a fire, sparked by two people at the center of all this chaos. They were...they seemed important, connected somehow. It felt ancient."

He stopped, taking a deep breath. Evelyn was silent for a moment, processing the vivid imagery Adrian had painted with his words.

"What does it mean?" she finally asked, her voice barely above a whisper.

Adrian shook his head, his gaze drifting to the window where the first hints of dawn colored the sky.

"I don't know," he admitted softly.

The room was quiet again, except for the distant sound of the early morning birds.

CHAPTER 2

EVELYN AND ADRIAN sat in the kitchen, hunched over their cups of coffee in silence, seeking comfort from the harsh realities of the outside world, as a gentle rain tapped against the window.

Three weeks had passed, yet the shadow of what had happened at the Dyeworks tannery before the explosion lingered over Baneford like a ghost. Ursula's team was gone, and their deaths now weighed heavily on Evelyn. Despite Adrian's attempts to push aside the creeping dread, she knew the deal she had made with the evil spirits, known as the Masters, would come back to haunt her.

Evelyn was more attuned to what was happening in town, through her career as a real estate broker. This was the first time in their relationship she felt danger looming before Adrian did. As a spiritual medium, Adrian didn't have the same connection to people as Evelyn did. Instead, he relied on his intuition and often communicated with spirits of the dead.

It was an ordinary Wednesday in May, yet nothing about their world was normal. Evelyn wrestled with a nagging sense of guilt for staying home while her agents were at the office, just days after sealing the deal on the apartment upstairs—a move that stretched her finances and pinned her hopes on a brighter future. After the sudden death of her upstairs neighbor, Mrs. White, Evelyn found herself unexpectedly responsible for selling the property. When efforts to sell it for Mrs. White's son were unsuccessful, he was willing to accept a substantial price cut. Evelyn got brave and made the purchase herself. She hoped it would prove to be a savvy business decision to generate additional rental income and lessen some of the risk associated with her commission-based job.

"This isn't what I expected," she sighed. "The rest of the world doesn't know. The town has no memory of what happened… But when I see people…like Trevor and Cam at the office, they have a haunted look in their eyes, as if they can feel they've lost weeks of their lives. And they can't explain the mysterious cuts and bruises. My deal with the Masters couldn't erase that. Wiping their memories didn't save them from the pain."

Adrian's voice carried a sharp edge, a rare note of contention between them. "You speak as if you expect dark spirits to honor their word," he said, his eyes narrowing slightly, a flicker of frustration passing over his face. "You should have expected this."

Evelyn's heart sank at the tone of his voice. *He's right*, she thought, *I was stupid to think we could make a deal with darkness.*

She put her mug down and sighed. He had never spoken to her that way before. After the danger subsided, the difficulties of being in love with a wandering spiritual medium from Romania, a vrajitaore, were clear. He had never lived in society or held a steady job. But he knew about dark magic.

"It's like the entire town is recovering from trauma. Even the real estate market here is dead. And it's booming everywhere else…" she added.

Adrian took a deep breath and paused, knowing he had been too harsh with his words.

"I'm sorry… I don't mean to sound angry. We won…we survived…and we have each other…we have a chance to build a life together, now. I think we should focus on that."

Evelyn could feel the resoluteness behind his words. A man who had traveled from across the globe to protect her.

"I know what I did hurt you," she confessed.

She wanted to accept the reality of what she had done, even though it had occurred in the heat of the moment without much thought or reasoning.

Adrian took Evelyn's hands in his.

"What happened at the factory...it was a horror... One we should have died in… But you saved us."

Evelyn looked back at him, replaying the harrowing memories of that night in her mind. Adrian had been inches from falling to his death, with Ursula standing at the edge of the crevasse, ready to kick him in. Driven by sheer instinct, Evelyn had snatched the knife from the ground and driven it deep into Ursula's eye. In that instant, the whispers of the Masters filled her ears, promising her anything she desired. Without hesitation, her heart accepted their offer. As a result, memories of Ursula's reign of terror were deleted from the town's collective consciousness, leaving only a select few who still knew the truth.

"What you did, it saved me," Adrian said, his voice softening.

In his eyes, she saw not just gratitude but a deep, unspoken understanding of the heaviness she now carried.

Since the explosion, one thing had become clear to Adrian. The voices of the dead that had always tormented him were gone.

"It's been three weeks, and my mind remains still."

Adrian's voice carried emotion as he spoke, because what had been broken so abruptly was a curse he'd carried nearly his entire life.

"Are you sure they're gone?" Evelyn asked.

Despite her regrets over causing him pain, Evelyn's deepest wish was for Adrian to find peace.

"I can feel that this is permanent," Adrian said. "When you risked your life to save mine, you broke the curse."

Adrian spent his childhood in the green expanses of Romania's rural countryside, where his mother Nadia passed down to him the ability to communicate with spirits. She taught him to listen and to understand the whispers of the dead—a legacy passed through generations. But when Nadia passed away, the gift she had left him became a burden.

The voices of the dead screamed for his attention, turning the silence in his mind into torment and anguish. To escape their relentless presence, Adrian turned his unique ability into a livelihood. He travelled the world, across all six continents, helping the living rid their homes of ghosts. Whenever he stopped, the dead would shout again, urging him to continue with his work. Reluctantly, Adrian accepted his fate as a devoted servant to these lingering souls, forever bound to the thin veil between life and death.

"You're free," she smiled back at him.

After more than fifteen years of roaming the world, Adrian found stillness, devoid of the suffering that had been his constant companion.

Evelyn was momentarily distracted by the sound of her cell phone ringing. She glanced down to see Mayor Jenkins's personal number displayed. With a hint of annoyance, she pressed the silence button, letting the call go to voicemail.

"Mayor Jenkins keeps calling me…asking if everything's okay…if we're safe."

Mayor Jenkins was one of the few who remembered the events at Dyeworks and had played a crucial role in concealing the truth of what happened, including the deliberate explosion that had brought down the factory.

"He saw too much," Adrian replied. "Most people cannot imagine what lies just outside their sight."

"At least there's some good news. He's managed to reappropriate the property back to town ownership by eminent domain, so the land and rubble that was Dyeworks isn't for sale anymore."

"That's good."

Adrian got up abruptly and headed into the living room, leaning against the windowsill to look out onto the street. Cars passed by in a steady flow, yet the sidewalks were empty because of the rain. When he heard Evelyn follow him into the room, he didn't turn to face her.

"I love you," Evelyn whispered, drawing nearer to him, sensing his somber mood. He was an outsider, not rooted in Baneford like she was, and his connection to the town was tenuous at best. For him, it had always been about her. She smiled, a mix of surprise and affection in her eyes. "I can't believe you showed up at my open house that day."

She could still clearly picture it, the intriguing stranger that shouldn't have been there.

"I was in Egypt when I first saw you in my dreams," he replied, speaking of the visions he'd seen before finding her.

The bond was out of the ordinary. Adrian wasn't drawn to the living. However, there was something about Evelyn that had captivated him, even before they met. Though she had no supernatural abilities, it seemed there was a special energy about her that attracted the paranormal.

"Why me?" she asked.

It was oddly a question that Evelyn had never asked before, and a topic that Adrian had never broached, but it was exactly what he needed to talk to her about now.

"I waited until I knew we could have a life to tell you this…this isn't our first life together."

She took a moment to process the strange statement.

"What do you mean?"

"You and I lived before…previous incarnations. I believe that is what I saw in my dream. It was a memory."

Her face twisted in confusion.

"I thought spirits got stuck here, or they moved on to…heaven or hell."

As she said the words, she realized they'd never talked about what happens after. *But there's something so familiar about him*, she thought. It had been that way since the first moment they met.

"So, are you saying that crazy dream actually happened? That was you and me?" Evelyn didn't know how to feel.

"I cannot say for sure. All of life comes in cycles, Evelyn. It is not a straight line," Adrian replied.

A knock sounded at the door in a rhythmic and playful tone, indicating it was a friendly visit.

"Casey," Evelyn whispered.

Out of the few people in her life, it was only her best friend who would show up unannounced. Evelyn went to the door to let her in.

"You have to see this!" Casey announced as she entered the apartment dressed in athleisure wear, and a grey windbreaker.

Her blonde hair was pulled back into a tight ponytail. She looked at them both sideways and then continued to the living room, grabbed the remote amidst a scatter of magazines on the coffee table, and turned on the television. Evelyn trailed behind her, as Adrian turned from the window.

Casey clicked to the local channel, where a news report was airing live coverage of an important scientific discovery in the woods near Echo Lake in Baneford. On the screen, they could see teams of archaeologists and their assistants maneuvering around one another in a designated area, carefully using brushes and picks to uncover hidden treasures in the soil. The unearthed artifacts were then delicately wiped clean, placed in labeled plastic bags, and sorted into sterile containers. In the background, vibrant green foliage signaled the arrival of spring, as the clouds parted, allowing sunshine to come through.

"Occultists and conspiracy theorists have long speculated that giants once roamed the Earth… But these giants, they're not just stories, like the tale of David and Goliath," explained the off-camera voice, his enthusiasm coming through the screen. "We might be looking at tangible evidence that they lived here over 20,000 years ago, right here in Baneford, Massachusetts."

Evelyn and Adrian looked at each other.

The reporter, dressed in a suit and tie, stood out amongst the backdrop of casually dressed academics engaged in their excavation work. As he spoke, one of the archaeologists crossed in front of the camera, cradling a surprisingly large bone in his arms.

"Excuse me, Dr. Slater," the reporter said to him, stopping him in time. "Would you mind saying a few words about what your team is finding here?"

The archaeologist paused, sweat and dirt visible on his forehead, then adjusted his grip on the elongated bone. "Regarding this," the archaeologist started, "we've excavated multiple skeletons, and this particular femur—observe its size—

it spans over three feet, far exceeding the standard for Homo sapiens."

"I think I know that guy," Evelyn mumbled, not taking her eyes off the TV.

"Sold him a house, perhaps?"

Adrian and Evelyn watched the screen with bewildered looks, but Casey's expression was closer to panic.

"Can you believe this?" Casey said, muting the television to speak. Her widened eyes reflected the flashing scenes on the screen in the blue hue of her irises. "Another freak show has come to town. They've been reporting on it all day."

Evelyn could see the fear in her friend's eyes, and she couldn't blame her. Casey had been through so much. Even the slightest mention of something out of the ordinary was now enough to send her into a negative spiral.

"It has been passed down in folklore and occult circles," Adrian explained. "Centuries ago, there were giants... Archaeologists are constantly making new discoveries; even in Egypt they have found lost temples buried beneath the sand. It doesn't surprise me—"

"But aren't you worried?" Casey interrupted. "I mean, with what's been happening in town the last several months…"

Adrian shook his head and gestured towards the television, where a helicopter view of the excavation site was now being shown.

"This doesn't mean anything other than finding more proof of what history is being kept from us."

Evelyn couldn't help but find this situation unusual. Adrian was always the one to alert them of any potential threats, and he just told Evelyn that they had known each other in a past life and had fought giants, so his disregard for the situation seemed out of character.

"That's a first for you," Evelyn teased. "You've never said things will be fine before."

Casey missed the irony and continued to stare wide at Adrian, waiting for him to confirm her worst suspicions. She expected him to say that evil was coming to Baneford again, and they would all somehow be caught in the middle of it.

I need to see this, Evelyn thought. *It's midday and there are policemen, TV crews, and scientists all around.*

"They're reporting live…we should go," Evelyn threw out. "There are a lot of people there—we'll be safe."

"I knew it," Casey grumbled, irritated by how quickly her friend was ready to jump back into a potentially dangerous situation.

Adrian had already shown his bravery and determination to confront any evil, engage in any battle, to protect Evelyn. After years of being imprisoned, he had finally gained the freedom to truly live. Yet that freedom already seemed overshadowed by the past.

"I will go with you," he said.

"Do you think it's safe?" Casey asked.

"The darkness I perceived before is gone." He was telling the truth, though feeling new misgivings.

"And what about the giants? What do you know about them?"

Her question carried the timid tone of a frightened child, prompting Adrian to pause and consider his response carefully. He then spoke in a gentle, low voice. "The stories say that they lived thousands of years before recorded history, long before the pyramids in Giza were built. They lived predominantly in the Middle East, in the regions of Anatolia and Mesopotamia."

"Were they evil?"

Evelyn's teeth pressed down on her bottom lip. She silently hoped that Adrian would say "no," regardless of what the truth may be, to ease Casey's fears.

"According to the mystical traditions that keep this knowledge, the giants civilized our ancient ancestors, but it came at a great cost. They are known as the Nephilim, or the Anunnaki. They taught humanity farming, animal domestication, astronomy, and how to build temples with monolithic stones. But they also sought to enslave humans. It's said that many among them became dark sorcerers before the time of the great flood."

Casey stared blankly at him, unable to fathom a response.

"So, they've been dead for thousands of years, right?" Evelyn said, eager to leave the apartment.

"Yes."

The news footage on the television showed a close aerial view of the dig site, capturing three large craters filled with an odd assortment of oversized bones.

"I guess I need to see this too," Casey sighed.

Evelyn grabbed her keys in a hurry, and they all made their way to her car. Adrian took the passenger seat, adjusting it to fit his tall frame. Casey climbed into the back, fastened her seatbelt securely, and began nervously tapped her fingers on her knees.

Evelyn took the familiar route south along the Washisund River, passing by the spot where they had stopped to watch the Dyeworks tannery burn after they'd set it ablaze. Adrian remained silent in the car, gazing out at the silhouette of industrial buildings on the banks of the river. Casey kept her focus on the road ahead, her eyes centered in Evelyn's rearview mirror.

As they neared the lake, the road curved and gained elevation, revealing a stunning view of the shimmering water below. Evelyn guided the car down the other side to the parking area. They saw it was filled with cars, including media vans and police vehicles. Finding a spot at the end of the lot, they stepped out of the car and crossed the road to the where the trails began, leading to where the excavations were taking place.

CHAPTER 3

AS ECHO LAKE receded into the distance, they ascended the path through the dense canopy of trees. Along the way, they encountered locals and a few reporters, all engaged in chatter about the excavation site. Despite her doubts, Casey couldn't ignore the beauty of the day. The rain had cleared, and the forest was full of vibrant colors, the sunlight creating a mosaic of light and dark on the ground. The higher they climbed, the more people they met descending, having already explored the site. Evelyn wondered how much busier the trail would have been on a weekend, considering most people were at work.

Casey and Evelyn, long-time residents of Baneford, both recognized the significance of the moment. In a town where noteworthy events were few and far between, limited to occasional house fires or business closures, this discovery was truly monumental. Significant occurrences had been scarce in Baneford since the early 1900s, when it thrived as a bustling hub for tanning and leather production, supplying top-quality materials across the country. However, those prosperous times had long faded, leaving behind only the memory. Now, Baneford stood as just another dilapidated town in northern Massachusetts near the New Hampshire border—more likely to contain subsidized housing buildings than ancient archaeological wonders.

"Are we allowed to just walk up to the dig site?" Casey asked, stepping over a fallen tree on their path.

"We're about to see," Evelyn answered, quickening her steps, with the gathering now coming into view not far ahead.

They noticed more locals and media personnel making their way down from the bustling activity further up the hill. Eventually, they arrived at a small assembly of about fifty people, situated roughly halfway to the summit. The area was secured with bright yellow police tape and ropes tied to stakes, marking out square sections for the ongoing excavation.

Three officers dressed in blue uniforms stood watch at the edges of the site, their main mission likely being to keep order among the curious spectators and to block attempts from reporters to sneak into the area the archaeologists were digging. They carefully monitored the boundary between the groups and kept a watchful eye on the nearby trees for any signs of suspicious activity.

Evelyn couldn't help but notice one particular officer—he had a round, bald head and a thick mustache, resembling her late friend Ed, killed in the violence at Dyeworks.

Approaching the crowd from the rear, the buzz of conversation grew louder. Evelyn listened in, catching snippets of speculation and theories about the excavation site.

"Maybe it's aliens," said a young man with spiky hair and large sunglasses, gesturing to his friends.

One of the observers, a woman in an orange sweater with a giant pot leaf on it, added her own theory to the mix.

"Nah, more Mother Earth vibes. It's like a sacred Native American site or something…"

Others had their own far-fetched theories, adding to the air of excitement surrounding the site. The hillside provided a natural amphitheater for the unfolding scene, centered around the excavation. Adrian, Casey, and Evelyn stopped behind the crowd, standing near where the underbrush gave way to the clearings for excavation. Behind the yellow police tape, the archaeologists and their helpers methodically worked with their tools while the residents of Baneford huddled together in small clusters, whispering their speculations.

After a short while, camera crews began to cluster around a figure approaching the perimeter of the excavation site. Curious townspeople edged closer, hoping to catch every word of the impending interview. The lead journalist, beaming with anticipation, positioned herself at the forefront, clearly eager for the opportunity to speak with the person in charge of the dig. The man, distinguished by a full head of silver hair and a natural tan, dressed in khaki pants and a cardigan. It was clear by the entourage and reception that he was highly regarded in the academic and research communities.

Adrian towered over everyone else, his dark features and sharp jawline giving him the air of a covert operative, even though he was dressed in a simple black t-shirt. To soften his imposing appearance, Evelyn reached out and took his hand, making him seem less out of place.

"Dr. Slater," the reporter began, his excitement coming through. "Your reputation precedes you, with a public career uncovering mysteries of ancient civilizations across the world.

Now, back in your native New England, how does it feel to be here today?"

"It's truly a pleasure," he said, flashing a charming smile at the camera. "This discovery holds immense significance not only for scientists in the U.S., but for all of humanity."

The audience leaned in to hear every word.

"You've been a steadfast proponent of the notion that giants once roamed the Earth, not merely the subject of fictional tales. After spending several days exploring this site, can we now conclude that your theories have been substantiated?"

The reporter, looking quite pleased with himself, held the microphone out to Dr. Slater to answer.

"I would say it's too early to draw conclusions, but the evidence certainly points in that direction," he stated cautiously. "I say that to honor the scientific community, who want to see evidence over conjecture."

He turned and signaled to two team members in white lab coats to approach. They carefully brought forward one of the sizable femur bones believed to be a part of an ancient giant's leg. The bone, weathered by time, was a deep, earthy brown hue and displayed an astonishing level of preservation.

"No, not that," Slater snapped suddenly. "The other one!"

The two colleagues shared a knowing look before making their way to a table far away from the caution tape. Resting on the surface was something sizable, hidden underneath a white sheet. Its shape was round and bulky, concealed by the fabric's folds. With a sense of reverence, they pulled back the cover to unveil a colossal skull.

Although it had a human-like shape, the skull was enormous, comparable to the size of a lion's head. Its empty eye sockets seemed to stare back at the shocked spectators, serving as a reminder of a long-past era that this small town knew nothing about. The colleagues lifted the giant skull from the table and carried it over to Slater. He reached out with steady hands and took it. The onlookers stood in silence, sensing the weight of this moment. Slater cradled it in his arms, like he was holding a baby.

"These beings once walked a world vastly different from our own. Long ago, during the last great Ice Age, the green hillside we see today was covered in ice, when woolly mammoths and saber-toothed tigers roamed this land."

"That is truly astounding," the reporter replied. "What has your team concluded about this fossil that you hold now?"

He swept one hand over the crown of the skull, as if connecting with the soul it once belonged to.

"This one was male, remarkably strong. I can sense the power that once coursed through him," Slater said with an odd display of certainty and longing.

Nodding to them, Slater beckoned his team members forward.

"Take it back," he instructed, relinquishing the skull back into their care.

The two team members carefully reclaimed the skull and returned to the table, placing the sheet back over it.

"What do you think this discovery might reveal as you continue your excavations here? Is there a possibility of finding more evidence of these ancient giants?" the reporter asked.

"I believe we're on the brink of uncovering far more than anyone can imagine. Our ground-penetrating radar scans have revealed the presence of structures buried beneath this hill. It appears to be a mass of stone blocks, forming what seems to be a chamber, and tunnels—a megalithic structure. Exploring what's there will require meticulous planning and time, but it's an incredibly thrilling prospect."

"Do you believe these colossal structures might have been constructed by the giants themselves?"

"Only time will tell."

The reporter nodded respectfully, concluding the interview. "Thank you for taking the time to speak with me, Dr. Slater."

In the background, a dedicated team of archaeologists meticulously sifted through buckets brimming with an assortment of bone fragments. Among them were vertebrae and teeth, potential puzzle pieces to the ancient mystery they sought to unravel. They painstakingly assembled the skeletal remains, their collective efforts aimed at reconstructing the forms of the giants who once roamed these lands.

Slater reconvened with his team in the middle of the site, and the journalist motioned for his cameraman to cut the recording. The crowd buzzed with excitement as everyone started speculating and exchanging new ideas about the discovery. Casey turned to Adrian once more.

"What about now?" she asked. "You saw the size of that skull…this isn't normal. None of this is normal," she rattled off anxiously.

Evelyn found it hard to conceal her frustration, taken aback by the dramatic change in Casey's demeanor. The Casey she knew had always been easygoing, athletic, and brimming with confidence. Now, she seemed perpetually on edge, which only intensified Evelyn's overwhelming feelings of guilt about being the cause of her trauma and suffering.

This time, Adrian was willing to lie.

"I don't sense anything," Adrian repeated, turning towards Casey to offer her a reassuring look.

In the midst of their exchange, they hadn't noticed Slater's departure from the excavation site until he was approaching them, heading toward the trail leading down the hill. Up close, he appeared taller. As he walked by Evelyn, he caught a glimpse of her face and suddenly stopped in his tracks.

"You must be with the *New York Times*." he said, extending his hand out to her.

Thrown off by the sudden gesture, she intuitively reached out and took his hand, only to tell him he had the wrong person.

"Sorry, that's not me."

With her long auburn hair, sparkling green eyes, and smart sport jacket, Evelyn looked every bit like a city reporter, which could explain why Slater initially mistook her for one. But standing beside her, Adrian couldn't shake the feeling that Slater had stopped for a different reason.

"You're not with the *New York Times*?" Slater said, his expression turning to confusion. "Have we met?" Evelyn did not like that Dr. Slater also felt like they knew each other.

"No, and I'm not a reporter. We're just here to see what's happening," Evelyn said politely, deliberately using the word "we."

"Maybe she sold you a house? She is Baneford's top real estate agent," said Casey, sounding more like herself.

"Well, I haven't lived in Baneford for a very long time. It feels like thousands of years ago." Dr. Slater chuckled. "Are you from around here, Evelyn?"

"I've lived here all my life…" Evelyn said, side glancing Adrian to make sure he was okay with her sudden conversation with the strange but friendly man. "I'm always interested in learning more about Baneford's history."

Slater's eyes lit up at mention of the word.

"Historians are in for an exciting time," he exclaimed. "Especially those interested in ancient history. Recent archaeological findings all over the globe are expanding our knowledge of human history, uncovering massive structures that go back even further than what we believed was possible before. We're talking long before Egypt, completely transforming our perspective on the beginnings of human civilization."

"How far back are these discoveries dated?"

"For the past few months, I've been conducting research at a remarkable location in Turkey called Gobekli Tepe. It's an incredibly impressive site, believed to be over 12,000 years old—just like the findings we're uncovering here. The ruins consist of circular stone structures, resembling temples, with intricately carved pillars, weighing nearly ten tons each, hinting to advanced civilizations that existed long before the reign of the pharaohs. This suggests that human civilization dates back much further than mainstream archeology claims and there may have been other pockets of civilization; all somehow sort of connected."

"That's incredible."

Left out of the conversation, Adrian looked away, his attention drawn towards a group of people walking up the hill.

"It's my personal theory," Slater said, licking his lips, "that we're going to find a connection between all these ruins, because unlike what traditional academics have taught us, our ancestors were powerful and capable of circumnavigating the globe."

The group Adrian was watching came into view—a camera crew headed by a woman in a professional suit. She quickly approached Slater and stopped directly in front of him, ready to engage.

"Mr. Slater, I'm glad we were able to catch you in time. I'm Brenda Myers with the *New York Times*."

"Nice to meet you, Brenda," Slater replied. "And nice to meet you as well, Evelyn, was it?" Slater didn't wait for a response before he excused himself from their conversation. "Brenda, I happened to catch that piece you did on Amir Zayne. Though I'm not his biggest fan," he added with a slight grimace, "I must say, it was an excellent piece of journalism."

"Well, if you're ready to proceed with photos and an interview, that's precisely why I'm here today," Brenda replied.

She motioned for him to join her and her team as they descended the hill, seeking out a quieter, more secluded spot where they could conduct the interview.

"He seems nice," Casey said, watching him leave.

Adrian and Evelyn also watched but didn't say anything.

For the next few minutes, they observed the other archaeologists diligently working beyond the yellow police tape. It soon became apparent that the day's activities were winding down. With nothing more to see, Adrian, Evelyn, and Casey decided to head back.

As Casey bounded ahead of them down the trail, Evelyn whispered to Adrian. "I never told Dr. Slater my name."

"I know. He said it twice."

As they descended the hill, they passed a small clearing in the trees where Dr. Slater was being interviewed by the reporter. As they walked by, Slater's eyes brightened upon seeing Evelyn, and he briefly paused his interview, his gaze lingering on her a moment too long. Then, finally turning his attention to Adrian, he flashed a grin that felt strangely familiar.

Once they had descended the steep hills, they strolled across the street to where their car was parked, near a police vehicle and several media vans. Evelyn drove them all back to the apartment, the air thick with silence. They stared out of their respective windows, lost in contemplation.

When they arrived, it was midafternoon, and their energy levels had taken a dip. They gathered in the living room, trying to process what they had just witnessed—undeniable evidence that ancient giants once lived in Baneford.

Adrian and Evelyn exchanged glances, eager to discuss her dream, the giants, and the charming Dr. Slater but not wanting to upset the already-fragile Casey.

"I should head home," Casey said after sitting in near silence for twenty minutes. She gathered herself, putting her windbreaker back on. "Please keep me updated on what you guys find out."

Evelyn rose and accompanied Casey to the door. There, she wrapped Casey in a comforting hug, trying to reassure her that she wasn't alone. After Casey left, Evelyn joined Adrian on the couch, looking stressed out.

"Are you alright?" he asked, brushing a stray lock of hair from her forehead.

"All that's happened—it's ruined Casey's life. And that makes me feel so guilty," Evelyn admitted.

"I understand," Adrian replied, taking Evelyn's hand. "But you can't blame yourself for what happened. You did what you had to do to protect yourself, and this town...and even Casey. It's not your fault."

Evelyn nodded, trying to take in his comforting perspective. "I just wish there was something more we could have done to prevent all of this."

"We can't change the past, Evelyn. All we can do is focus on moving forward and do our best to make things right." He pointed up at the ceiling. "Any applications to rent the apartment?"

"Not yet."

He wrapped his arms around her, and they shared a silent understanding to push their fears aside for a while. The world of ghosts and giants could wait, while they relished these brief moments of happiness, just as anyone else would.

CHAPTER 4

THE NEXT MORNING, sunlight filtered through the curtains of Evelyn's bedroom, bathing the sheets in a soft light. As Evelyn and Adrian lay together, they would have loved to remain in what felt like a peaceful cocoon, but their thoughts inevitably drifted back to the giants and the implications of the discoveries at Echo Lake.

Propping himself up on one elbow, Adrian spoke the first words of the day.

"Casey is anxious to know if evil is coming to Baneford. It's something you and I both need to know."

"I would like to know if your dream was just a dream or if I need to be anxious too."

"There's a ritual I can perform to find out if the dream was a memory, then we might not have anything to worry about. But it was a vision; a premonition, then we have battled giants before and won. So maybe we don't need to be so scared…of giants or anything else?"

"What kind of ritual?" Evelyn asked, wiping the sleep from her eyes.

"I will tell you later. I must prepare first."

Evelyn lay beside him, a thoughtful expression in her eyes. She found herself at a loss for words to fully express how extraordinary Adrian truly was, with how much he knew about things no one else spoke about.

"I need to head to work today," she said, giving him a kiss on the cheek before getting out of bed. She restrained herself from asking any questions, knowing that the answers would be waiting for her when she returned home.

Despite the sluggish pace of Baneford's real estate market, Evelyn headed into the office that morning to support her agents and uphold a semblance of normalcy during these uncertain times. However, she would have greatly preferred the comfort of her home over fulfilling her duties as managing broker that day.

With the caffeine from her morning coffee pulsing through her veins, Evelyn hurried through her dressing routine, her thoughts racing faster than she could button her blouse. She left the apartment while Adrian was still writing a list of items he needed for the ritual that evening.

As she drove to her office in Baneford, she navigated the familiar streets while contemplating the tough spring market ahead. It seemed like just yesterday that her career and financial prospects were promising, but now, with that promise fading, she faced the possibility of everything collapsing.

Evelyn parked her car on Main Street and strolled down the familiar path, passing by storefronts that held cherished memories from her childhood. However, those memories were now tainted by Ursula's dark influence, and the awful, depraved things she made people do.

Walking up to the glass window of her real estate office, she stopped for a moment. The once bold and eye-catching black and gold letters spelling out "EM Realty" now looked dull and unimpressive. She peered inside, spying on her agents Cam and Trevor at their desks. They both appeared exhausted and defeated, reflecting the decline in business.

As a young female business owner, Evelyn was acutely aware of the ever-shifting dynamics around her. It wasn't just the sluggish real estate market that concerned her now, she also sensed a growing fear among the town's residents. As she had told Adrian, the town was traumatized, and she wondered how long this condition would persist. She tugged on the glass door and stepped into the office, forcing a smile to mask her worries.

"Good morning, team. How's it going?"

Cam, Trevor's young Vietnamese assistant, spoke in a whisper so faint it was barely audible.

"Good morning."

Although typically reserved, Cam's effectiveness as a transaction coordinator made her an invaluable member of the team. Trevor gave Evelyn a brief nod, his usual meticulously maintained appearance now replaced by a haggard look, with his blonde hair unkempt and his dress shirt wrinkled and untucked. The tough real estate market and recent turmoil in the town were taking a visible toll on Trevor, who usually thrived on the excitement of new deals and listings. Cam's behavior towards him had also changed. She used to eagerly follow his lead, but now there was a noticeable reluctance, likely a result of his mistreatment of her under Ursula's influence. Although they both couldn't remember what happened, their changed attitudes showed the lasting impact of what had occurred.

The absence of two key agents significantly altered the atmosphere of the office, a change that Evelyn felt keenly. Blake had taken an extended leave after encountering a haunted listing—an experience that shook him deeply. However, the more profound loss was Sheila, who had been gruesomely killed in the recent cult activities.

As soon as Evelyn sat down at her desk, she felt the overwhelming urge to get up and leave. She pushed herself to come up with something to say to her agents.

"Any new business, or friendly conversations this week?"

Cam responded with evident frustration. "We've sent out a hundred mailers, called past clients, door-knocked, everything…" she whined. "Even the listings we had signed are starting to cancel. We need to expand outside of Baneford and focus on new zip codes, or we're not going to make any money."

"We have a territory!" Trevor interjected angrily, his tone making it clear that this was a familiar point of contention.

Evelyn, sensing the escalating tension, tried to smooth things over. "Let's consider the idea," she suggested gently. "Exploring new areas could open up opportunities we've been missing."

Trevor shook his head vehemently, signaling to Evelyn that further discussion was futile. She resigned herself to the rest of the morning, which she spent absorbed in her computer screen, meticulously sifting through emails and updating her CRM by removing contacts of clients who had moved away or passed on. Her last transaction had involved acting as both agent and buyer for Mrs. White's apartment, and with no active clients left, what she did now felt futile.

By one in the afternoon, Evelyn was ready for a lunch break and headed down to the Fairhaven Diner. As she sat at the counter, her restlessness lingered as she gazed out the window, observing the slow pace of the world outside. Returning to her office, she still felt drained and anxious, with the temporary rise in blood sugar doing little to improve her overall sense of unease.

Trevor and Cam also took a break for lunch, but they ended up staying out longer than usual. When they finally returned, they simply slumped back into their chairs. Evelyn understood that the problems they were facing now stretched well beyond the walls of their office. By the time four o'clock came around, Evelyn had already decided she'd had enough for the day.

"I won't be in tomorrow," she said, getting up from her seat. "Have a good weekend."

Evelyn grabbed her purse and headed towards the door. As she left, only a vague grunt from across the room reached her ears. The glass door shut quietly behind her. Walking to her car, she heard her cell phone ring. Seeing the name on the display, she let out a sigh before answering.

"Mayor Jenkins?" Evelyn answered, her tone polite but lacking the deference she once held for him.

"Good afternoon, Evelyn. I hope I'm not interrupting your work."

"No, I just left the office. What's going on?"

She got into her car and plugged the phone in, switching to hands-free mode.

"I need to discuss something important with you," the mayor said nervously. "Can you come to my office?"

Reluctantly, she agreed, partly because of how unproductive she felt.

"Okay, I can be there in fifteen minutes."

"Thank you, Evelyn. I'll see you soon."

Evelyn drove to Baneford Town Hall, situated in a well-maintained neighborhood that stood in contrast to the rest of Baneford. The sidewalks here were tidy, the lots were spacious, and the lawns were impeccably manicured. After parking her car, she approached the grand entrance of the town hall. The security guard at the front desk acknowledged her with a nod.

"Good afternoon, Ms. May. The mayor is expecting you," he said, gesturing towards the staircase. "You can go right up."

Evelyn ascended the stairs to the mayor's office and gently pushed open the slightly ajar door. The room came into view, lined with tall bookshelves filled with leather-bound books with gold lettering. Wide bay windows framed a view of the street below.

Inside, Mayor Jenkins sat at his mahogany desk, deeply engrossed in his work. Papers were strewn about, and the soft glow of the desk lamp accentuated the stress lines on his forehead. Upon her entry, Mayor Jenkins looked up and acknowledged her with a nod. Evelyn walked over and took a seat across from him.

"Hi, Mayor, what's going on?"

Mayor Jenkins put down the stack of papers he was reading through.

"There's been an uptick in real estate activity here. It seems some off-market transactions are happening."

"Really? My office has been quiet."

"It's a series of LLCs purchasing properties on Main Street, adjacent to Dyeworks, and a few others down the street."

"That's...unexpected," Evelyn replied. "I'm surprised anyone's buying here."

"The town can't legally refuse the sales," Mayor Jenkins explained. "They're with the registry of deeds. However, any demolition permits will have to be approved here, by me."

"You can't let anyone we don't know get access to those tunnels under Dyeworks. We don't know who else knows what Ursula knew."

The thought of another person like her arriving in town and casting spells on the residents, sacrificing them to the Masters was too overwhelming to process so soon after what had happened.

"Most of the properties facing and abutting Dyeworks are owned by old Baneford families," the mayor said defensively, hiding a hint of guilt for letting these deals slip through. "Next of kin have mostly moved away, so I doubt this buyer will be able to snatch up anything else."

"Let's hope so," Evelyn said, thinking to herself, *what an idiot.*

"What about you and Adrian? You see anything strange on your end?" he asked, changing the topic of conversation.

"We went to look at the excavations at Echo Lake. Ancient giants in Baneford thousands of years ago. I assumed that's what you called me in for. We don't know if it's connected to anything…we saw the bones, and a bunch of excited archeologists."

"You have no idea how good this news is," the mayor said, slapping his desk once for emphasis. "That's the one good thing we have going on. Academics and scientists are pouring in. We're getting media attention. It's a huge international discovery. We need new money and new blood in this town, and this could help us."

Evelyn looked through the window at the street below, daring to hope that the town could still make a comeback.

"I think we need more than that… What about the company buying properties here?" Evelyn asked, refusing to let the previous conversation dwindle.

"I won't allow any more sales to go through until we learn more," he assured her, before she left.

Evelyn arrived at her building ten minutes later. Upon entering her apartment, she found the lights dimmed, with a soft glow emanating from the living room.

Inside, Adrian had rearranged the furniture to make room for their ritual. He had laid out a thick hemp rope around the room's inner perimeter, forming a rectangular boundary. The decorative items had been carefully moved aside, and the coffee table was pushed against the wall, creating an open space in the center of the room. In the middle of this space stood an antique mirror on a stand, its brass edges tarnished and the glass slightly discolored.

"I met with the mayor today," Evelyn said as she moved further into the room, stepping over the rope.

"Why?" Adrian asked, looking up from his preparations.

"He mentioned that an unknown company is buying up properties on Main Street, near Dyeworks."

"We'll need to find out more about that."

Evelyn glanced around the room one more time.

"What's all this for?"

"The rope helps to contain the energy of the ritual," Adrian explained, while rummaging through his duffel bag.

He pulled out a collection of stones and crystals—some rough and jagged, others polished and smooth. Carefully, he selected two large stones, black tourmaline and onyx, and placed them at the center of the marked space. He then distributed smaller amethyst stones around the room, setting them on bookshelves, the TV stand, and the windowsill.

"These will create a powerful energy flow," Adrian explained, lighting a stick of incense, and the room filled with the scent of sage.

"Are you ready to start?" he asked.

"Just give me a moment to change," Evelyn replied, slipping away to her bedroom.

She returned shortly, now dressed comfortably in her nightly T-shirt and sweatpants. She noticed that Adrian had thoughtfully arranged two pillows on the ground in front of the mirror, setting them next to each other. He gestured toward them, inviting her to sit down.

"Don't worry. We are only voyaging through memory tonight. Nothing will come through this time," he assured her, a reference to the first séance they performed together.

Evelyn settled next to Adrian, their knees touching. Adrian lit three candles he had positioned in front of the antique mirror, casting flickering shadows across their faces.

"I want you to look into the mirror, and when you're able, join me in the chant," he instructed.

Evelyn inhaled deeply, allowing her body to relax and be present in the moment. *Here we go again.*

Adrian began the chant in Romanian, his voice low and bassy, the words resonating deep within his bones. Each syllable vibrated through him.

"Străbuni... Luminați-mă... Străbuni... Luminați-mă!"

Evelyn felt the reverberations too, each one penetrating deeper into her consciousness. The chant continued, and the resonant vibrations drew her further into the ritual. Fully immersed in the moment, she joined Adrian, their voices harmonizing.

"Străbuni... Luminați-mă... Străbuni... Luminați-mă!"

They repeated the chant over and over, and as they did, the room seemed to pulse with energy. Staring into the mirror, their reflections began to swirl in a kaleidoscope of colors, revealing something entirely new. What they saw was beyond what Evelyn could have imagined possible.

As if from above, they saw an ancient city on the water, its architecture characterized by concentric circles and towering pyramids at its center. Closer in, was an oval temple constructed of large granite blocks. Inside and outside the enclosure, men and women who looked from an age long past stood watch, keeping a lookout on the horizon.

"What is this?" Evelyn asked.

"The past," Adrian replied.

Within the temple walls stood a man and woman standing within a megalithic stone enclosure. They had their palms facing the sky, enacting a ritual. They spoke, and the stars in the night sky above seemed to twinkle brighter in response.

"Who are they?"

"Keep looking."

The images in the mirror shifted again.

On the horizon, what these ancient people dreaded appeared. Massive figures emerged, sprinting towards the entrance of their stronghold. Though they bore a resemblance to humans, they stood over ten feet tall with wild, unkempt beards and rugged, savage features. They were adorned in otherworldly armor.

Evelyn's heart weighed heavily as she sensed the gravity of what happened long ago.

The people from the temple fought against the giants, trying to keep them from getting inside as the man and woman continued with their incantation.

Before they could witness the outcome of the impending clash, the mirror shifted abruptly, its surface swirling into a new scene. Waves of emotion from a life lived thousands of years ago swept over Evelyn, infusing her with a profound sense of sadness.

Under the light of the moon, a ship rode the turbulent waves of the open ocean. Water crashed all around from the storm. Above, the stars were hidden behind thick clouds that raced across the night sky, blocking out the moon's illuminating glow. A group of people pushed against heavy oars, straining to keep the vessel on its intended path. The man and woman were among them, gazes locked onto the horizon, holding on for life.

And then, just as suddenly as it had appeared, the vision dissolved, leaving Evelyn breathless and bewildered. She found herself staring back at her own reflection and Adrian's in the mirror. The flickering candlelight cast shifting shadows across Adrian's face as she turned to look at him.

"You were right," she gasped, her voice trembling slightly, "we have lived before?"

"I suspected," Adrian replied, his tone sorrowful. "I didn't want to mention it in case…the pain of remembering our past and then being separated would have been too much."

"We were fighting giants. And I think we're destined to relive the same terrible fate," Evelyn said, looking him dead in the eyes.

CHAPTER 5

AS THE SUN made its slow descent over Main Street, Saul Griesmeyer and his associate, Cavil Stern, proceeded along the sidewalk, less than a quarter mile from the Dyeworks factory, pausing at each address. They surveyed the boarded-up windows of the storefronts and dilapidated duplexes lining the desolate industrial district.

After weeks of diligent work, they had successfully acquired multiple properties in the area, but their primary target was the old Dyeworks factory site and the properties surrounding it. This area, once the bustling center of the town's industry, now stood as a haunting reminder of its former glory. The streets were dirty, the pavement uneven, and the abandoned factories, with their crumbling facades and broken windows, echoed memories of a time long past.

If not for his formidable associate beside him, Saul might have been mistaken for a wealthy man who had accidentally wandered into a rough neighborhood. Slender and of average height, he wore a well-tailored suit that hinted at affluence. Sparse grey hair at the sides of his otherwise bald head indicated his advancing years. Standing next to him, Cavil presented a stark contrast—tall and intimidating, with a full head of black hair, a square jaw, and the flat, hardened face of a boxer. He clutched a leather folder filled with blank offer letters and purchase contracts.

"Mark that one down," Saul instructed, gesturing toward a building with rusted metal numbers above its entrance.

The presumably once lively Italian restaurant now bore clear signs of abandonment, with boarded-up windows and a sign marred by graffiti. Cavil opened his folder and began writing. In the background, the clattering of metal carts on uneven pavement filled the air. Shadowy homeless figures in tattered clothing drifted out of the darkness, moving silently down the narrow alleyways between buildings.

"How much do you want to offer for this one?"

"Half a million. Let's make sure they don't hesitate when they see our offer."

Cavil completed the necessary details on the form and passed it to Saul for his signature. Once signed, Cavil deposited the document into an age-worn mailbox affixed to the building's exterior. Saul then gestured towards another building further down the street, one they had not yet approached with an offer. Together, they resumed their journey up Main Street, methodically repeating their process as the day gradually wore on.

Eventually, they arrived at the site of the abandoned Dyeworks factory, now a desolate field of rubble. The factory, known for its iconic brick facade, had been devastated by a fire and subsequent explosion, fueled by flammable lacquer in the tanning drums. Now, the site lay cluttered with heaps of concrete, twisted metal, and scattered bricks.

A green construction fence surrounded the remains of the factory, acting as a barrier between the wreckage and the rest of the town. Saul gestured through the fence towards a massive mound of rubble and dust, where various remnants of machinery and the factory's structure were haphazardly piled up.

"That's where she died," Saul said, peering in.

Cavil closed his eyes, taking a deep breath to connect with the dark memories of the site.

"There were many sacrifices to the Masters here," he added, and then began coughing violently.

He pulled a handkerchief from his pocket and used it to wipe away the blood that came up.

"Are you okay, sir?"

"Not yet..." Saul said, pausing to catch his breath, "But I will be. Once we open the portals, I'll be renewed in my health, and I will give you everything I promised."

Cavil looked at Saul with a mixture of respect and loyalty.

"I know, sir. I'm here till the end...to help us both."

The disheveled figures loitering in the alleys behind the deserted factories paused abruptly at the sight of the two men approaching. They quickly pushed their carts away, disappearing into shadows, eager to evade any confrontation or potential encounters with law enforcement.

Saul and Cavil approached a discreet black Lincoln Town Car parked at the curb. Cavil took the driver's seat while Saul settled comfortably into the back. They drove away from the dilapidated industrial sector towards the opposite end of Main Street, where the environment transformed into a bustling commercial area.

"I want to buy something on this side," Saul said as they neared the livelier part of town.

Cavil parked the car in front of a retail store, marked by a red and white sign that read "Lucky's Hardware." The shop windows displayed an array of gardening tools, paint cans, and power tools. Inside, through the glass, bins filled with nuts, bolts, and screws were visible, along with various other home improvement tools.

As they stepped into the vintage store, the scent of sawdust and metal greeted them. Behind the counter stood Tim Moulton, the late Mr. Moulton's son, a young man in his 20s with a faint mustache. He welcomed them as they entered, but they ignored him, absorbed in their own conversation.

"How much?"

"Half a million."

Cavil opened his leather folder and filled out a new offer sheet and placed it on the glass counter in front of Tim.

"Good evening, gentlemen," he said, staring down at the sheet of paper. "What's this?"

"An offer to buy this store. Business and real estate," Saul said.

Tim had recently inherited the store following his father's untimely death in the town's recent chaos and was startled by the unexpected offer.

"Who says I'm selling?"

Saul stepped forward to the counter. "Your father passed recently, didn't he? I would think you'd rather take the money than try to make this miserable shit your dream," he said, gesturing about the store.

"You knew my father?"

"I'm glad to say I didn't," Saul replied callously.

"Selling wasn't what I had in mind," said Tim, clearly taken aback by the remark.

Cavil reached across the counter, seized Tim by the collar, and slammed his head down onto the glass counter. He pressed his face against the hard surface, pinning him down with one hand while twisting his arm behind his back with the other. Tim struggled beneath Cavil's grip, his face grimacing in pain as he tried to free himself.

"What do you want?" he squealed.

"Take the offer," Cavil said, then let go.

Tim picked up the offer letter from the floor, his hands trembling as he placed it on the desk. Breathing heavily, he reached for a pen and signed the offer.

"You'll hear from my attorney," Saul smiled.

Cavil snatched the document, and without another word, he and his boss walked out of the store and returned to the car.

"Are you heading home now, sir?" Cavil asked as he closed the driver's door.

"No, take me to the mayor's house first," Saul instructed.

Cavil turned the key in the ignition, and they began their drive along Main Street. They passed the Fairhaven Diner, the public library, and smaller retail storefronts, including a bridal shop and an ice cream shop. One window caught Saul's attention, where "EM Realty" was prominently displayed in bold letters.

"That's her office," Saul remarked, nodding towards the brokerage office.

Cavil acknowledged with a brief nod and redirected the car toward the upscale part of town where the mayor's house was located. As they drove further, the neighborhood transitioned to one of increasing affluence—houses here boasted well-manicured lawns and pristine white picket fences.

At the end of a quiet cul-de-sac, the mayor's house stood out as a charming two-story brick structure topped with a sleek black slate roof. Cavil parked the car in front of the garage, and they both approached the front door. Cavil knocked firmly three times.

The door gradually swung open to reveal a woman clad in a sheer T-shirt that accentuated her long legs. The ring on her finger confirmed her identity as Mrs. Jenkins, a young brunette whose youthful appearance made it clear that the mayor had married someone much younger. The transparency of her shirt left little to the imagination. Her face registered surprise, obviously not expecting company. Inside, the foyer was illuminated by track lighting, which, combined with the soft classical music, created an elegant atmosphere. Further down the hallway, the dining room was well-lit, suggesting that their arrival had likely interrupted the couple's dinner.

"Can I help you?" she asked politely.

"We're here for him," Saul said dryly.

Mrs. Jenkins left the door slightly open as she hurried down the hallway through the French doors to the dining room. She returned shortly, Mayor Jenkins close on her heels. His dress shirt was unbuttoned, and his tie loose. As he approached the door, he saw Saul's gaunt face peering through the narrow opening and a towering figure beside him.

"Who are you and what do you want?" Mayor Jenkins demanded sharply, poised to call the police.

Saul pushed the door open further and stepped inside.

"My name is Saul Griesmeyer. I've been buying properties along Main Street, and I'm here to talk about Dyeworks."

Ignoring the stunned silence from Mayor Jenkins and his wife, Saul and Cavil walked past them into the dining room. They took seats at the table, where the mayor and his wife's dinner was growing cold. After a moment of hesitation, Mayor Jenkins reluctantly followed them without reaching for his phone.

"Don't worry, everything will be okay," he reassured his wife, signaling for her to leave them alone.

"Should I call the police?" she whispered.

"No," he replied, understanding that if these men were anything like Ursula, the police would not be helpful.

Mrs. Jenkins's expression turned to one of dismay as she quickly scurried down the hallway, disappearing from sight. Taking a moment to steady himself, Mayor Jenkins then entered the dining room. He settled into his seat at the opposite end of the table, directly across from Saul, who had taken over the spot where he had been eating dinner minutes before.

"We are in the process of expanding our property ownership in your town," Saul began, his tone firm and businesslike. "So far, we have acquired four properties surrounding the old factory. I need to secure the Dyeworks site as well."

The mayor exhaled deeply, his features reflecting the relentless stress of recent weeks. Each day brought new crises at town hall; remnants of the chaos Ursula had sown throughout the town. He was still haunted by the vivid memories of townspeople being attacked by small, crimson-red demonic creatures, and he still struggled to accept that his former assistant, Stewart, had conspired behind his back to make these things happen.

"I knew someone would come after Ursula," he said, the fatigue evident in his voice. "But I can't sell you Dyeworks."

"That's not an option!" Saul screamed, banging his fist on the table. "Ursula had a vision, one that I've come to fulfill."

"Who was she to you?"

Saul paused, then abruptly succumbed to a fit of harsh, ragged coughs. When he pulled his hand away from his mouth, there was blood on his palm. He quickly wiped it away with a handkerchief.

"She showed me what real power is," he said, putting the blood-stained cloth back in his inside suit pocket. "And that's what I've come to claim…"

"There are people in this town who will stand against you," the mayor replied, side-glancing at Cavil, wondering who would win if he and Adrian were to fight.

"If you're talking about the real estate agent and her Romani boyfriend, I know exactly who they are. They won't get in the way of my plans because I know things Ursula did not, and I know what you did to cover up what really happened."

The mayor was consumed with anxiety about the potential ruin of his career and life if the truth were to come out. After Evelyn's encounters with the Masters, only a handful of people, including himself, were meant to know the full extent of what had happened.

"Show him the map," Saul instructed.

Cavil nodded and promptly hurried out to the car, leaving the front door ajar. He reappeared shortly after with a laptop in hand and placed it on the dining table. He clicked the mouse pad a few times, then turned the screen towards the mayor, revealing a detailed map of Baneford. All streets, zones, landmarks, and conservation areas were clearly displayed.

Saul made his way to the opposite side of the table and pointed to a spot on the screen.

"This is Dyeworks." Moving his finger across the screen, he added, "And over here are the ongoing excavations at Echo Lake," pointing to the area surrounding the foot trails.

The mayor noted the proximity of the former factory to the lake excavations, something he'd failed to take in before.

"Are you suggesting these places are connected somehow?"

"Both are along the Washisund River," Saul said with a hint of impatience. "These are ancient settlements that date back further than you can imagine. They belong in the hands of those who know what they are."

Suddenly, Cavil seized Mayor Jenkins by the neck and forcefully slammed his head onto the table. The mayor's nose broke with a crunching sound, sending blood streaming down his face. Cavil then let go, and the mayor slumped back, groaning in pain.

"If you don't sign it, I'll kill you," Saul said, patting the mayor on the back.

As Saul and Cavil exited the room, the mayor was left alone, cupping his nose, with blood pouring down onto the tablecloth. The sound of the front door slamming brought the mayor's wife running into the room, and she immediately let out a piercing scream at the sight of his battered face.

CHAPTER 6

AFTER THE RITUAL, Adrian restored the living room to its normal state. Evelyn remained seated on the floor, lost in thought. The intensity of the ritual had drained her emotionally as well, leaving her feeling empty. Adrian coiled the hemp rope and set it aside, then carefully packed the crystals into his duffle bag. He moved around the room, rearranging the furniture, sliding the coffee table back into its original position, and pushed the antique mirror back against the wall.

Evelyn slowly rose from the floor, clutching her cushion tightly against her chest. Adrian gestured toward the couch.

"Come, sit down."

Evelyn eased herself down next to him, hugging the cushion close as she leaned in, pulling her legs up and resting her head in his lap. He began to stroke her hair as she played the visuals from the ritual once more in her mind.

"What does all that mean?" she asked.

Adrian looked down into her turbulent green eyes, reticent to tell her what he suspected.

"The visions showed us that we fought against giants. And the excavations at Echo Lake now seem connected to our past… An echo of something from long ago."

Evelyn's eyes widened.

"An echo of what?"

"I don't know."

"And does this have anything to do with the Masters?"

"I don't know that either…"

Evelyn's eyes filled with tears in an instant. She blinked furiously, trying to hold them back, but the overwhelming emotion consumed her. She could still feel the desperation of her past life, the fear that both the man and woman had endured.

"I feel it too," Adrian said. "We were different people…but it was still us."

"There was so much fear in her heart."

Adrian's eyes deepened with empathy. "Now we understand how our souls knew each other…and I love you," he said, reminding her of something good to hold on to.

"I love you too…" Evelyn replied. "But we both know something's coming."

"Yes." Adrian understood that time in the spirit world was cyclical, and if they had faced evil in a past life, it was likely to reemerge. The thought of losing Evelyn terrified him, but he refused to let these fears consume him entirely. "I've spent my entire life wandering the world alone. I won't let anything happen to you."

Evelyn could hear the genuine emotion in Adrian's voice. As someone who had lost both her father as a child and her mother as a young adult, Evelyn was no stranger to loneliness and feeling disconnected from the world.

"I was alone too... And you are my family now," she said.

He ran his fingers through her hair, again and then gently lifted her face up for a kiss.

Evelyn sat up and quickly shed her shirt while Adrian slid off her pants, both driven by a deep need to connect. Standing to remove his own clothes, he paused to admire the sight of her, then sat back down, so that Evelyn could straddle him. This time felt different, intensified by a deeper spiritual understanding. As they moved in perfect rhythm, an overwhelming sense of euphoria surged through Adrian, and then Evelyn, bringing them both toward ecstasy.

Afterwards, as they lay together on the couch, Evelyn nestled in Adrian's arms, she gradually returned to her senses. Yet, despite the warmth and comfort, there was a lingering sadness in her heart.

We're going to lose each other, she feared, her heart thumping in her chest. Looking back on her life, Evelyn saw scars etched into every chapter. She had endured loss, battled demons, and saved herself from certain death. *I just want to start over*, she thought.

"Maybe we should think about leaving this place," she said. "Sell the business, rent the apartment, and leave."

"There are many places I could show you," Adrian replied.

"Where?"

She traced the lines of his chest, running her fingers over old scars.

"We should go spend a few months with my friend Maruf in Egypt," Adrian suggested.

"I'd love to see Egypt!"

He could tell by the look in her eyes she wasn't joking. Evelyn's mind immediately raced through the steps she would need to take to leave Baneford—informing her agents, listing her business for sale, and preparing for an extended period without income. She found herself questioning whether she had the resolve to completely uproot her life.

"It seems impossible when I think about all the things I'd have to do…and the idea of not having a job…will you be able to make money?"

"I have no problem making money when I need to," he reassured her. "But you don't need to figure it all out now. If you want to get out of town, let's start with something easy."

The suggestion sparked a glow of relief and excitement in Evelyn's eyes. She stood up and began to dress herself.

"How about we go away for a couple of days? How about New Hampshire?" she said, tossing Adrian his shirt. "Casey and I used to stay at a nice place in the White Mountains called the Bartlett Inn. We can go hiking and stay there for the night. I can invite her too…"

Adrian smiled, picturing it.

"That sounds perfect."

Evelyn reached for her phone to call her best friend. With the recent chaos in their lives, she believed Casey deserved at least a weekend getaway as well.

"Hey, Casey, how about we go hiking in New Hampshire tomorrow morning? It'll be good for us, fresh air, nature, just a day or two away."

"That sounds like a great idea."

Evelyn arranged for them to meet at her place the next morning at 10 AM and drive together in one vehicle. She hung up the phone, relieved that Casey had agreed to join them.

As they relaxed together, Evelyn and Adrian discussed the places they might visit once her business was settled. Adrian talked about the Himalayas, the beaches of Australia, and the incredible food along the Amalfi Coast. The conversation ignited Evelyn's thoughts about leaving Baneford, giving her plenty to ponder as they finally retreated to the serenity of their bedroom at the end of the day.

***

The morning after their visit to the mayor's house, Saul and Cavil stood on the shore of Echo Lake. The still waters mirrored the blue sky and surrounding trees. From their position at the lake, they could see down the path to the road below, and nearby, another trail led up into the hills where excavations were ongoing. After a few moments, Stewart, the former assistant to the mayor, emerged from the direction of the road, making his way up the trail toward them.

Stewart approached with his usual fidgety and anxious manner. His hands twitched slightly at his sides. Despite no longer being employed by the town, Saul had summoned him here because Stewart had been a witness to all of Ursula's influence, the dark rituals, the sacrifices. As he walked up to them, he peered at Cavil, tilting his neck back to take in his full stature.

"I don't know what you want from me. Dyeworks isn't for sale anymore," Stewart said, pulling a crumpled letter from his jacket pocket that he had received. "After the explosion, the factory was taken back by eminent domain."

In the letter, it was clear that Saul had inside knowledge about all that had happened, even making reference to Stewart's family ties with the factory going back centuries. Stewart didn't know who Saul actually was or how he had acquired such detailed information, and he would have rather avoided this encounter altogether. But a threatening ultimatum at the end of the letter left him no choice but to attend and those words repeated in his mind now. *If you don't come, I'll find you, and I'll kill you.*

"My name is Saul Griesmeyer," he said, snatching the letter from Stewart's hand, crumpling it, and tossing it to the ground. "I know you're no use to me with the factory. I brought you here because I need information about the woman and her friend."

Stewart's frustration burst forth.

"I hate them. He did this to me," he said, taking off his glasses to show the fresh scars that were visible on his face. "And she's a bitch."

Stewart glanced back at Cavil again, his looming presence triggering memories of Adrian towering over him, pummeling his face with his massive fists.

"Ursula made the mistake of underestimating them. I won't do that," Saul said. "And I don't care what they did to you."

With a subtle cue from Saul, Cavil's hand shot out, firmly grabbing Stewart by the collar, yanking him abruptly toward the trail. "Move!"

Saul lagged behind as they trekked up the trail, his occasional coughs echoing in the background. After five minutes and about 100 yards from the lake, Cavil abruptly led Stewart off the path and into a clearing hidden by trees. With a sudden shove, Cavil sent Stewart stumbling backwards, causing him to land on a pile of twigs and tree bark.

"Why did you do that?" he shrieked.

As he brushed off the debris from his clothes, Stewart noticed Saul discreetly coughing up blood into his handkerchief before quickly concealing it.

"You know what they found here, right?" Saul said, breathing heavily, pointing up the hill to where the excavation site was.

"You mean the news about the giants?" Stewart replied.

"See how little you know… They were powerful beings from another dimension, sorcerers with immense power. You know them as the Masters…"

"The Masters were giants?" Stewart's confusion was evident.

"Their time came to an end after the great flood, but their souls remain tethered to the earth by the strength of their magic. And I will bring them back."

Bringing himself to his feet, Stewart peered up the hill in the direction of the excavation site. In the distance, he could see someone on the main trail rapidly descending towards them. As he got closer, they could see that he was leaping from one foot to the other, using gravity to propel himself. He slid to a stop right where they had veered off the trail and stepped in through the trees. The person was an older man in his fifties, wearing a dress shirt and tweed jacket, but moving with the agility of a much younger man.

"Good morning, gentlemen," Dr. Slater greeted.

Even though it was still early, the sweat on his forehead and the layer of dust on his clothes indicated he had already been working at the site for some time. But it was clear that he had been eagerly anticipating this meeting.

"He's the one who arranged the sale to Ursula," Saul said, pointing to Stewart. "And he knows them."

Slater took an object out of his pocket.

"I hear they're something special," he said, rolling a battered gold coin between his fingers. The metal was etched with concentric circles on both sides.

Stewart stared at the strange coin, unsure what to make of it.

"I want you to tell my friend everything you know," Saul said.

Stewart nervously began to speak, eventually telling Slater everything he knew about Evelyn and Adrian and what happened with the Masters.

At 10 AM, Casey pulled up to Mox Street and found a spot to park her car. She quickly made her way into the building, heading straight for Evelyn's door. When it opened, Evelyn was greeted by the sight of her friend dressed in outdoor gear, fresh and bright-eyed. It was a reminder of how Casey had been, before all the awful things that happened.

"You want some coffee?" Evelyn asked, gesturing towards the kitchen.

"Sure."

In the kitchen, Adrian looked up from his seat at the counter and reached for the coffee pot to pour a cup.

"So, what's the story behind this hike?" Casey said, taking the cup and moving to the fridge to add some milk.

"We haven't been to the Bartlett Inn for years, and I thought it we all deserved a little getaway. Plus, I wanted to show Adrian the White Mountains."

"Oh, the croissants at the inn are to die for," Casey remembered fondly. "If I ever date again, we should make it a foursome." Her mind wandered. "You guys are so lucky to have found each other."

"Oh, Casey. You'll find the right guy, sweetie. I promise." Evelyn pulled Casey into a hug.

"Well, I can always just tag along with you guys. The perpetual third wheel," Casey said into Evelyn's shoulder.

Exchanging a glance, Adrian and Evelyn hesitated. They didn't want to unsettle Casey with their plans to permanently leave Baneford. The hike was meant to be a temporary escape from town, while they figured out how to relocate permanently. For now, a short trip to New Hampshire was the immediate plan, a small step towards their bigger goal. But Casey's comment made Evelyn think it would better just to rip off that band-aid.

"I've been thinking about leaving Baneford," Evelyn admitted.

Adrian took a small sip of his coffee and stayed quiet, letting Evelyn handle the situation with her best friend.

"What? Leave Baneford? Why?" Casey was visibly hurt. "Hold on. What's going on Evie? What did you find out?"

Evelyn glanced at Adrian. "We don't know much, but you were right… We are connected to the excavations somehow… We saw it in a vision…"

"A vision? What do you mean? What did you see?" asked Casey, even more agitated.

Evelyn searched her mind for the appropriate details to disclose. "I'm so sorry, Casey."

"Let's not worry about this now," Adrian interjected. "It's something I think we should discuss later."

"But, you said there was nothing to worry about, Adrian."

Casey eased onto a stool and inhaled deeply, placing her mug gently on the counter, as her mind raced through everything she and Evelyn had been through together, especially the last several months. Adrian and Evelyn didn't speak, allowing her to process the little information she'd been given.

Casey emerged from her thoughts and looked Evelyn right in the eyes. "You know, I'm with you till the end, Evie," she said. "No matter what."

Feeling a deep sense of gratitude for her loyal friend, Evelyn hugged Casey tightly, expressing her affection in the most heartfelt way she knew.

"Thank you, Casey. I love you so much."

"I love you too. But stop it now," Casey said, pulling away, "you're gonna make me cry. Come on. I'll drive.."

After a few moments spent gathering themselves, they were ready to leave the apartment. They grabbed their bags by the door and made their way outside.

At her blue SUV, Evelyn took the passenger seat and Adrian squeezed into the back, positioning himself diagonally to accommodate his long legs. Casey turned the ignition, and they set off on their drive to New Hampshire, playing soft blues on the radio. The interstate cut through vibrant greenery, with the fresh scent of spring wafting in through the open windows. They passed quaint towns and sprawling dairy farms, taking in the views of rolling pastures and meadows. However, not long after they crossed into New Hampshire, Evelyn began to feel nauseous.

"Pull over," she announced suddenly, her tone urgent and uncomfortable.

"Are you okay?" Casey asked, glancing over.

Nodding frantically, Evelyn pressed a hand to her mouth, signaling was going to throw up.

Casey quickly took the next exit off the highway and found a quiet side street. The moment the car stopped, Evelyn swung her door open and vomited on the side of the road. Adrian stepped out, offering a bottle of water and some tissues.

"Are you alright?" He asked.

Evelyn wiped her mouth, nodding as she took a sip of water.

"Yeah, I'm fine now. Sorry, I don't know what that was about."

After making sure Evelyn was okay and settled back in her seat, Casey put the car into drive again and navigated back to the highway. Adrian kept his eye on Evelyn for a few minutes, before settling back into staring out the window.

After a little over three hours of driving, they arrived at the inn. The charming exterior welcomed them, standing out against the dense forest that enveloped it. Towering trees dotted the property, casting pockets of shade on the ground under the hot afternoon sun. Casey parked, and they collected their belongings from the car before going inside.

Upon entering the inn, a young man with fiery red hair and freckles welcomed them and swiftly checked them in at the front desk. Taking their keys, Evelyn and Adrian proceeded to their room, while Casey settled into her own across the hall. They quickly prepared for their hike by packing a few water bottles and extra layers should it get cold. After regrouping in the lobby, Casey passed out granola bars for a quick boost.

With plenty of daylight remaining, they set out on the dirt path that began just fifty yards from the hotel, snaking their way through the forest and up a lush green hill. The trail ascended a steep slope, weaving through dense woods, over twisted roots, and past tree stumps. Adrian led the way,

Casey maintained a steady pace, her backpack securely fastened as she maneuvered through the rugged terrain. As the path twisted deeper into the dense forest, Evelyn began to lag behind. Although they were only a quarter of the way up, the enthusiasm with which Evelyn had started the hike was visibly dwindling, replaced by an increasing sense of anxiety. Adrian and Casey, leading the way, frequently glanced back at her. They noticed a distinct tension in her posture and the sweat on her forehead, which was unusual given the coolness of the air hadn't caused them to perspire. Evelyn's expression had shifted to worry, her eyes continually darted around, as if she expected someone to attack them.

Lost in her thoughts, she didn't see the twisted root stretching across the path. Her foot snagged on it, causing her to stumble and fall with a loud thud. Laying on the ground, tangled in leaves and dead branches, she let out her frustration.

"Fuck!" she screamed, her voice echoing through the trees and down the mountain.

They knew something was wrong.

"Hey, Evelyn, you okay?" Casey asked.

Adrian knelt down beside her, offering her a hand up. "Did you hurt yourself?"

Evelyn knocked his hand away, shaking her head. "Don't touch me!"

Evelyn's sharp reaction caught Casey and Adrian off guard, but she didn't seem to care. She got up from the ground and started walking up the trail, leaving them behind, not bothering to turn around. Confused, they followed her for a few minutes, trying to understand what had caused her sudden shift in attitude.

She seemed to have found her rhythm, but when she suddenly stopped and turned around, her condition startled them. Her eyes were bloodshot, her clothing drenched in sweat, and white foam had collected at the corners of her mouth.

"Evelyn," Adrian called out with concern, "you don't look well." Catching up to her, he reached out and placed his hand on her forehead. "You're hot…"

"Don't worry about it," she said, knocking his hand away a second time.

"He's just concerned for you," Casey interjected. "I am too…"

"Stop complaining," Evelyn snapped. "I'm sick of how weak you've become."

Casey's face went pale at her best friend's uncharacteristic behavior. The forest seemed to go silent around them, and then, a moment later, embarrassment washed over Evelyn.

"I'm not feeling well…" she muttered.

From where they stood, they had a view of the valley below, with the sun hanging low in the sky. There were beads of sweat rolling down Evelyn's face and neck, her shirt sticking to her skin. Irritably, she took off her outer layer and tied it around her waist, in an attempt to cool down.

"I think we should turn around," Adrian suggested, beginning to think Evelyn was dealing with more than just fatigue.

"I wish you never came to Baneford. We're all going to die because of you!" she screamed, another wave of anger moving through her.

"Evelyn, please," Adrian whispered calmly. "This isn't like you."

Evelyn shrieked and lunged at Adrian, trying to take him down, but he was quick to react and caught her, wrapping his arms around her to keep her from falling or hurting herself. Casey's eyes welled up with tears as she watched. After a few moments, Evelyn's frantic movements ceased, and she went limp in Adrian's hold. He lowered her to the ground where she lay still to rest.

"We need to get her home," he said.

After a brief ten-minute break, Evelyn started to regain some of her energy. Her eyelids fluttered as she lifted herself up with their assistance. She had a slightly embarrassed expression in her eyes but didn't say anything as they helped her walk down the mountain, supporting her weight from either side.

The return journey was difficult, especially for Evelyn, whose strength had diminished. She trudged between Adrian and Casey, her breaths heavy and sporadic, trying to maintain balance on the uneven trails. By the time they reached the inn, the temperature had dropped, and the sky was turning dark, with the inn's lights shining as a beacon to guide them back.

Adrian assisted Evelyn into the backseat of the car, draping his sweater around her for warmth. Inside the inn, Casey handled the checkout process and collected their belongings. Returning with the luggage, she loaded it into the SUV, and climbed into the driver's seat for the long drive home.

Crossing stateliness, Casey looked in the rearview mirror at Evelyn, then at Adrian.

"Should we take her to a hospital?"

"I'm fine now," Evelyn interjected. "I just want to go home."

Adrian kept quiet, turning to look at her, and saw that there was noticeable improvement in her condition. Her complexion had regained some color, and she sat upright, indicating that some of her energy had returned.

Upon reaching her apartment building, Casey parked the car across the street and Evelyn immediately opened the door and stepped out into the cool evening air and walked inside her building. Adrian got out to get the bags from the back and walked around to Casey's window. She rolled it down.

"What's happening to her?"

"I don't know… But I will find out."

CHAPTER 7

AS THE WARM water flowed over her skin, Evelyn felt her illness slowly dissipate. By the time she stepped out of the shower, she felt like a different person. The exhaustion and paleness were gone, replaced by renewed vitality. Her wet hair hung softly around her face, and her cheeks were flushed from the hot water.

"I don't know what got into me," Evelyn said, drying her hair with a towel.

"I'm not sure," Adrian replied, leaning in the doorway with a concerned look.

The illness had come on suddenly and disappeared just as quickly, making him wonder if it might have been something paranormal. Evelyn noticed his worried expression.

Adrian entered the room and began to pace back and forth, his movements taking him from the foot of the bed to the window. Meanwhile, Evelyn changed into comfortable sweatpants and a T-shirt before sitting on the edge of the bed.

"I'm so sorry for what I said to you," she said, recalling the harsh words she'd screamed at him during her moment of illness.

"You weren't yourself."

He sat next to her, gently moving her damp hair behind her ear. She leaned into him, appreciating the quiet moment together after their disastrous first attempt at having fun away from Baneford.

"I said something awful to Casey too…"

Evelyn took a moment to reflect on her earlier outburst, then quickly reached for her phone. After a few rings, Casey's weary voice answered the call.

"Hello?"

"Hey, Casey, it's me."

"Evelyn… Are you okay?"

"I just wanted to let you know that I'm alright now."

There was a moment of silence on the other end.

"You sure? I dropped you off less than an hour ago."

"Yeah, I'm okay…"

"You scared us, Evie. I know something evil is happening. It's not your fault."

"Thanks. We're going to figure this out, Casey," Evelyn said.

"Just take care of yourself. Let Adrian know he can call me if he needs anything."

Casey hung up the phone and Evelyn stood there for a moment trying to convince herself that what had happened was not connected to the Masters. Looking to wind down, Evelyn silenced her phone, set it on the dresser across the room, and then got into bed. Adrian followed suit, and once they were both settled under the covers, she reached for the remote on the nightstand and turned on the TV.

As she flipped through the channels, searching for something to take her mind off things, she came across the local news station, still covering the ongoing excavations at Echo Lake. The segment displayed images from ground-penetrating radar, showcasing intriguing circular stone structures buried under the hill. The scans hinted at a vast network of ancient ruins waiting to be discovered.

Evelyn and Adrian sat in silence, both silently acknowledging that the discoveries at Echo Lake could potentially bring unwanted changes to their lives. Once the news segment was over, they sat in contemplation for a moment before turning off the television and lights. Despite the uncertainties of the day, they both wished to sleep and for the day to be over.

***

When the morning light filtered into the bedroom, Evelyn woke from her sleep, burdened by yesterday. She had hoped to leave Baneford and start anew, but lying in bed, she couldn't help but wonder if the town would even let her go. With a heavy heart, she pushed aside the covers, trying to muster some glimmer of hope for the times ahead.

The thought of facing the outside world was daunting. She made up her mind that she would remain at home, away from the office and the rest of the outside world. Her resolve strengthened with each step she took towards the living room and that's where she saw Adrian, sitting on the couch, lost in thought.

The sudden ring of the phone startled them both, causing Adrian to sit up from his relaxed position on the couch. Evelyn rushed to the bedroom to retrieve her cellphone, then returned to answer it.

"Mayor Jenkins," she said, her face falling in disappointment.

"Evelyn, I need Adrian's help," the mayor said, his voice coming through loudly.

"What's wrong?"

"My house," he answered. "There's something here. I feel it. Please tell him."

Evelyn looked at Adrian and rolled her eyes, silently conveying the message.

"I'll talk to him about it, and we'll get back to you."

A smile spread across Adrian's face as Evelyn hung up the phone. Despite his mixed feelings about the mayor, he couldn't help but feel a certain sense of importance that he was personally being called upon for his services.

"What should I ask him to pay?"

"As much as you can," Evelyn replied with an exasperated breath, conveying her own dislike of the mayor ever since the events at Dyeworks.

"But I won't be calling him today," Adrian said, shaking his head. "I have something else to do."

He stood up, grabbed a cushion from the couch and tossed it onto the floor before sitting down on it.

"What are you doing?"

"Meditating," Adrian replied, crossing his legs.

Evelyn decided to let Adrian be and returned to her bed. She dozed off, drifting in and out of sleep until it was noon. When she finally got up for the second time, she headed to the kitchen and made herself a strong cup of coffee before going to the living room, only to find it empty. She could hear the sound of typing coming from her office. As she entered, she was taken aback to see him using her laptop.

She lingered in the doorway, watching him work. As the caffeine began to kick in, she glanced at her watch and decided she still had time to accomplish something productive today.

"I'm heading into the office for a bit... What are you up to?" she asked, her curiosity piqued.

"I'll fill you in later," Adrian replied without looking up.

With a brief and reluctant nod, Evelyn left to get dressed, her thoughts quickly turning to the day's tasks at the office.

She drove through the familiar streets of town, her mind preoccupied with plans and projects, until she reached Main Street and parked her car. As she approached her office building, Evelyn could see her colleagues through the large glass windows. Inside, Cam was at her desk, scrolling through property listings, while Trevor was at the copy machine. Entering the office, Evelyn forced a smile to greet them both.

"Morning," Evelyn said. "You guys killing it today?"

"It's dead," Cam muttered.

Trevor nodded in agreement. "I heard a rumor that the Dyeworks explosion was linked to some bizarre cult," he said, catching Evelyn off guard with his statement. "You know anything about that?"

Evelyn's heart jumped, but she remained composed. "That sounds like nonsense. Just rumors, I'm sure."

Evelyn gave an awkward nod, hoping to end the conversation, and made her way to her desk. After a while, her grumbling stomach reminded her it was time to eat. She walked down Main Street to the Fairhaven Diner for a quick meal. When she returned, she was surprised to find someone waiting for her—an elderly woman with silver hair and a warm smile.

"That's Mrs. Sanderson. She's here for the rental," Trevor shouted from across the room.

Evelyn smiled politely at the woman and sat down at her desk. "Would you like anything to drink? Coffee, tea, or water?"

"No, thank you," the woman replied, clutching her purse with wrinkled hands. "I'm interested in the apartment you have for rent."

"What brings you to this apartment, Mrs. Sanderson?"

Mrs. Sanderson's reply was laced with a hint of melancholy. "I recently sold our home in Old Bedford. My husband passed away, and it's just too much space for me now. I'm looking for something smaller, easier to manage."

Nodding sympathetically, Evelyn handed her an application form. "I'm so sorry to hear about your husband. The apartment, as I'm sure you saw from the listing, is a three-bedroom, one-bath on the second floor. You're okay climbing the stairs?"

"Yes," Mrs. Sanderson responded, taking the form, and filling it out.

After Mrs. Sanderson handed back the completed application, Evelyn quickly reviewed it.

"You seem like an excellent fit. Please give me a few days to run a credit check and get a lease drawn up."

"Thank you, dear," Mrs. Sanderson said, rising from her chair. "I look forward to your call."

She waved goodbye warmly and walked out. Watching her leave, Evelyn felt optimistic about her new potential tenant and the prospect of reliable rental income—a step closer to her plans with Adrian.

At 4:45 PM, Evelyn organized her desk, straightening papers and filing them away to clean up the clutter. Before leaving, she called Casey to invite her over. Once Casey agreed, Evelyn grabbed her bag and headed for the door.

"I'll see you both tomorrow, Cam and Trevor," she called out as she left the office.

Evelyn then got into her car and drove home. Upon reaching her building, she entered and found Adrian still engrossed in his work on her laptop in the office.

"Are you going to tell me what you're working on now?" she asked, hanging her jacket and purse on the coatrack.

"Planning a trip with you." Adrian said, looking up with a devious grin.

"A trip?"

"Do you remember the friend I told you about?"

"Maruf...the Egyptian exorcist?"

"He's much more than that," Adrian smiled. "I had to spend some time tracking him down. He doesn't always carry a phone, and he wasn't in his home in Egypt. I learned that he travelled to the Canary Islands, off the coast of Morocco."

The names of exotic places teased Evelyn's sense of adventure.

"I've always been curious about him from your stories..."

Adrian's jaw clenched as his expression turned serious. "We're going to have to face what's coming, and I need guidance. The things we saw in the ritual...your sudden illness...the discovery of the giants... He can help me make sense of all of this..."

Evelyn sat down at the other side of the desk, and he slowly lowered the laptop screen.

"Is there any room for fun?"

"It's a tropical island. I'm sure we'll be able to be tourists. But when I finally reached Maruf, he told me to come right away, and that the timing was preordained."

"Let's go," Evelyn said enthusiastically.

A knock at the door interrupted them.

"Hold that thought," she said, rising from her seat and returning with Casey by her side.

"Casey. Is everything alright?"

"I didn't see any giants, if that's what you mean," she half joked. "I thought I'd stop by on my way home and see how Evie was feeling."

"I feel totally normal. Must have been the flu."

There was a long pause.

"What are you guys doing?" Casey asked.

"We're planning a trip, actually," Evelyn replied. "A vacation."

"Now we're talking. Where?"

Adrian swung the laptop around and moved to the other side of the desk.

"We're going to see my old friend, Maruf, in the Canary Islands. Come take a look," he invited, gesturing towards the screen.

As they gathered around, Adrian pulled up a series of stunning images of the region. The screen displayed vibrant photos of pristine sandy beaches, rugged mountains, and ancient volcanic craters, each more breathtaking than the last.

"That is exactly what you two need. I'm so happy for you." Casey didn't let her trepidation show.

Adrian clicked to another tab, showing a different set of pictures of white stucco buildings nestled along a tranquil coastal stretch.

"This is where Maruf is staying, in the quieter part of the island. It's not fancy, but it will be clean and comfortable."

"I hope you find the answers you're looking for," Casey said. "And I'm really glad you're going together."

"He's helped us before," Adrian replied, acknowledging Casey's intuition.

Casey and Evelyn went into the living room, giving Adrian the space to concentrate on organizing the trip. For the next hour, he remained in Evelyn's office, diligently booking their flights and accommodation. Meanwhile, Casey and Evelyn settled into a comfortable conversation on the couch. During their chat, Evelyn shared what she knew about Maruf—a spiritual medium from Egypt renowned for his ability to exorcise dark spirits.

When Adrian finally stepped out from the office, he found Casey was already getting ready to leave. He walked them to the door, and that's where she placed her hand on his shoulder.

"Take care of her, okay, Adrian?"

"I always will."

"Will you be okay while we're gone?" Evelyn asked, concern in her eyes.

"Absolutely. I have three new clients this week. I'm so busy, I won't even have time to help you choose what bathing suits and outfits to pack."

As Casey turned to leave, she looked at Evelyn.

"Despite everything that's happening…that is happening…I really hope you have some fun."

As the door closed, it occurred to Evelyn that for someone accustomed to a life of travel, the prospect of travelling again was probably comforting to Adrian. More than that, she sensed his desire to share his experiences with her, things very few people could understand.

CHAPTER 8

ADRIAN AND EVELYN'S trip arrived quickly, with only two days between booking their flights and departure. Adrian decided it was best to put off any meetings with the mayor until after they returned, wanting to avoid any potential problems. Meanwhile, Evelyn took those two days off from work, using the time to plan out her beach outfits and taking a break from the stresses and routines of everyday life.

Evelyn informed her co-workers about her upcoming absence by email. She wanted to put all of her energy into preparing for the journey ahead, rather than worrying about the work she would miss. Her main priority was letting Mrs. Sanderson know that she had secured the apartment and that her application had been approved. Evelyn took care of this task the night before they left, sending an email with a copy of the lease and promising to meet with her upon their return.

The day of travel, they were packed and out the door before sunrise, their suitcases ready and their apartment securely locked behind them. Eager to leave Baneford behind for a few days, they hailed a taxi and headed to Logan Airport. As they crossed the Zakim Bridge, Boston's skyline gradually emerged, the skyscrapers catching the early morning light in a beautiful display. *I can't wait to see this new place*, Evelyn thought, watching the view from the window.

The airport was a chaotic scene, filled with people from all over the world and announcements of distant destinations booming through the speakers. Adrian led the way, weaving through the busy terminal. Once they passed through security, they searched for the correct counter to check in for their Portugal Air flight. The check-in process was smooth and quick, leaving them with some time to unwind before boarding. They took advantage of this by enjoying coffee and pastries in the airport lounge. Evelyn then walked over to a nearby newsstand and bought a *National Geographic* magazine to read during the flight.

The plane taxied along the runway, gradually picking up speed until it lifted off into the sky. As the plane ascended, the landscape of New England shifted into a stunning mosaic of clouds and earth stretched out below them. Evelyn and Adrian engaged in light conversation while peering out the window as they soared higher. However, as they settled into the flight, with the turbulence easing and the seat belt sign turned off, Evelyn began to feel restless. She pressed her hand against her forehead, feeling unexpectedly feverish.

Within minutes, Evelyn's discomfort escalated sharply. The queasiness in her stomach and a rising sense of irritability made it increasingly difficult for her to maintain her composure. She attempted to breathe through the discomfort quietly, but the symptoms only intensified. Feeling increasingly unwell, she shifted restlessly in her seat, struggling to find some relief.

"I don't feel that good."

"What's wrong?" Adrian asked, looking back from the window.

"I'm not sure. I feel anxious in my body, like everything's closing in around me."

"Maybe it's just the takeoff of the flight," he said, taking her hand. "But you do feel hot."

Evelyn reached for her National Geographic and began to flip through, though she could hardly focus on the words, tapping her foot anxiously as she turned the pages. Adrian kept a watchful eye on her, but she felt so terrible that she closed her eyes and leaned back in her seat for the remainder of the journey, refusing to eat any of the in-flight meals. Eventually, she was able to sleep the last four hours of the flight. Adrian, unable to relax now, alternated his attention between Evelyn and the window, where he watched the seemingly endless Atlantic Ocean pass below. *Maybe this was a mistake,* he thought to himself.

As the plane began its descent into Lisbon, Evelyn was abruptly awakened by the jolt. She felt the dampness of her clothes clinging uncomfortably to her skin, and her fever seemed to have returned with a vengeance. Adrian, noticing how pale she looked, became increasingly concerned. He helped her gather their belongings once the plane reached the terminal, taking charge of both their carry-ons. Evelyn leaned on him for support, struggling to maintain her balance on the way to the connecting terminal. She found the strength to find the restroom and change into a dry shirt. Afterward, they found empty seats near their gate, where she could recline and rest.

"Evelyn, do you think it might be a good idea to go back to Baneford?" Adrian asked with sincerity in his voice.

Evelyn hesitated, torn between her desire to continue and the toll her illness was taking on her. She paused to gather her thoughts.

"I don't want to give up yet..." she whimpered, trying to gather her strength.

Adrian gave a nod of acknowledgement, admiring her determination. With their minds made up, they boarded the next flight, hoping that the warm subtropical weather at their destination would help Evelyn heal.

During the two-and-a-half-hour flight to the Canary Islands, Evelyn's condition deteriorated rapidly. Her illness triggered an increase in irritability. Throughout the flight, she found herself grumbling about the cramped seats and the incessant drone of the airplane, continually venting her frustrations. Each outburst was followed by moments of lucidity, during which she recognized her behavior and felt ashamed.

"I'm sorry, Adrian. It takes over."

"It's not your fault. I should not have booked a trip so soon after you became sick the first time."

As the flight neared its end, the aircraft began its approach to the Canary Islands. Gradually, the descent started, and the plane aligned with the runway. The wheels screeched as they hit the runway, causing Evelyn to shudder from the impact. She leaned heavily on Adrian for support as they navigated through customs. Her steps were shaky, and her fever showed no signs of subsiding.

Stepping out of the airport, they were greeted by the warm island breeze, but it was hard for them to fully appreciate this long-anticipated moment. Amidst the bustling crowd, Adrian's eyes searched until they finally spotted Maruf and pointed him out to Evelyn. Maruf was an of average height with distinct Nubian features, sporting well-groomed black hair and a tidy beard, framing his face. It was quite a change from the last time Adrian had seen him in Egypt, when he was dressed in traditional garments as a tribal chief. Now, away from his duties in his southern Nile village, Maruf was dressed in casual Western clothing, fitting right into the island atmosphere.

"Thank you for meeting us."

"It is my pleasure, my friend." His welcoming smile and warm eyes shifted to concern as he took in Evelyn's visibly fragile state.

"We should move quickly," Adrian said. "She needs rest. Maybe a doctor too."

Maruf guided them out of the chaotic arrivals area of the airport. He had rented a Wrangler, with its doors removed, for an unobstructed view of the island. As they drove off, they passed beautiful beaches, lush greenery, and lively local scenes. The road along the coastline offered stunning views of the ocean and the cliffs, then changed to rolling hills dotted with palm trees. The sun shone on their faces, and the salty breeze brought the fresh scent of the sea. Evelyn, despite feeling unwell, lifted her head to enjoy the view, finding a moment of relief in the scenic drive.

After twenty minutes, they arrived at their hotel. Maruf maneuvered the car to a stop in front of the quaint three-star hotel. Its simple yet inviting design featured pristine white walls and a traditional terra cotta roof that exuded a warm

Mediterranean vibe. Working as a team, Maruf and Adrian unloaded the suitcases and brought them inside the lobby. Evelyn linked her arm with Adrian's for support as she entered, instantly relieved by the cool blast of air conditioning against her overheated skin.

Adrian escorted Evelyn to the designated seating area, ensuring she was at ease before proceeding to the check-in counter. He checked on her intermittently as he presented their reservation details and passports to the receptionist. Once everything was confirmed, Adrian received the keys to their room and turned towards Maruf, who had been waiting patiently for them.

"I'll take her to our room now."

Aware of the seriousness of the situation, Maruf nodded in agreement.

"I'll stay here and wait for you," he said calmly.

Adrian led Evelyn down a hallway that branched off from the main building, eventually bringing them outside to a line of cabins situated by the ocean. Despite its modest size, their cabin was charming and had a small patio with breathtaking views. Weary and feverish, Evelyn collapsed onto the well-made bed, but she soon found herself shivering under the covers as she tried to rest through her physical discomfort.

Sitting beside her, Adrian gently stroked her hair.

"Try to rest."

She nodded weakly, her eyes closing. "Thank you."

The crashing waves in the distance blended with Evelyn's deepening breaths as she slowly drifted off to sleep.

Adrian's thoughts were turbulent as he walked back to the lobby, where Maruf was waiting. Upon seeing Adrian, Maruf stood and motioned for him to follow to an outdoor cafe by the waterfront. The place had a few tables covered in simple tablecloths, serviced by a single waiter. Adrian sat down across from Maruf; his expression clearly distraught.

Maruf signaled the waiter and ordered two cups of tea for them. Adrian, looking dejected, had envisioned a proper introduction between Evelyn and Maruf, his only real friend. Over the years, Adrian had shared his deepest struggles with him. Now, faced with new challenges, Adrian knew he needed to turn to his friend again for guidance.

"I'm worried about her. She was fine when we left, but now I'm sure the further we are from Baneford, the worse she gets. The last time she was sick like this, we had left her town."

"But you're not taking her to a doctor…so you must know this is not a medical issue," Maruf replied.

"She has been involved with blood magic." Adrian let the words ring alone for a moment. It was unavoidable. "…but I'm certain now her suffering is connected to it."

"Let her rest for a while, and then I will check on her," Maruf said. "The spirits of Baneford are far from here, and this island has its own energies."

As they sipped their tea, Adrian shared a detailed account of the recent events that had gripped Baneford—everything from the dark spirits of the Masters to the violence and chaos at the

Dyeworks factory before the explosion. He then told him about the excavations at Echo Lake, and the artifacts and structures that had been found. Maruf listened intently, his eyes widening at the mention of giant bones.

"Like I mentioned on the phone, you're coming here now seems preordained, because this place has connections to the beings you are speaking out."

Adrian took this opportunity to inquire why Maruf had made the impulsive decision to journey solo to the Canary Islands. As a spiritual leader in his Nubian community in southern Egypt, Maruf held great responsibilities, so his reason must have been significant.

"Why are you here now?"

"These islands have a connection to ancient Egypt... Twelve thousand years ago, there was a great civilization here that sank under the waves. These islands were mountaintops in a land you may have heard of called Atlantis."

"Atlantis?" Adrian asked.

Despite a lifetime of dealing with the supernatural, he had still considered it to be nothing more than a myth.

"Those ancient ones who survived the flood, settled near the rivers of the Middle East—the Nile, Tigris, and Euphrates—restarting civilization. My people trace our origins to here."

Adrian stared at the vast blue water in front of him.

"I didn't know it was real..."

"There was a time when giants and other supernatural beings lived. All the religions have their flood stories…when God chose to wash away the wickedness from the earth…"

"Wickedness?"

"They became evil when they used blood magic to try to live forever…and where there is darkness, there must come light," Maruf said, looking into Adrian's eyes.

As Maruf shared his knowledge about Atlantis and its giants, Adrian immediately thought of the past life visions he and Evelyn had seen. The connections to their recent archaeological findings in Baneford suddenly made sense. Everything seemed to have a purpose now. He took a deep breath and told his friend about the visions they had seen.

Maruf listened intently and then told Adrian why he had come.

"I'm here for a ritual, one that originated before the great flood. It's a practice preserved by the ancient Egyptians and handed down through generations to me. Tomorrow night, an alignment of magnetic and astronomical forces will occur, opening a portal. This is the same portal that the giants used to come here, thousands of years before recorded history. Everything is connected, and it's no coincidence destiny has brought us together now."

As they chatted, the sun gradually lowered on the horizon. The light reflected off the water, shimmering in the distance. Eventually, Adrian started to feel like they might have lingered too long, so he invited Maruf to accompany him back to the room and check on Evelyn.

"You might be able to see what I cannot."

Maruf nodded in agreement and followed Adrian back to their cabin. Entering, he saw Evelyn lying on the bed, sleeping with a pained expression on her face, her auburn hair damp from fever and matted against her forehead. Maruf approached the bedside and stood in silence, looking at her. He then extended his hands, hovering them inches above Evelyn's body, feeling for the disturbances in the energy around her. After a moment of quiet concentration, Maruf gently lowered one hand down on her forehead. He could feel the heat radiating from her, and Maruf sensed that this was no ordinary illness.

"There is indeed the presence of many dark spirits surrounding her."

Adrian's shoulders slumped, though this only confirmed what he knew already. "Is there anything we can do to help?"

Maruf shook his head. "This is a consequence of what she has done. Her soul is tethered to them now, and it seems the further away she is from her home, the more painful they will be. Allow her to rest for now. Tomorrow night, the ritual will show us the way forward."

Maruf slipped out of the room, gently shutting the door behind him.

Adrian undressed and slipped into bed beside Evelyn. In the silence, he was acutely aware that soon, something or someone would come for them. He listened to the sound of Evelyn's breathing for hours, thinking of ways they might defeat evil once more, until finally sleep came to him.

CHAPTER 9

EVELYN WOKE UP to sunlight peeking through the blinds, finding herself in an unfamiliar room with a ceiling fan above her. Her voice came out hoarse and filled with frustration as she spoke.

"Why didn't you wake me up?"

She looked no better, her hair disheveled and her skin pale. Adrian recounted the previous evening's discussions with Maruf, including the ritual planned for later that night. He explained that Maruf, upon learning about their encounters with the Masters and the events at the Dyeworks factory, firmly believed their coming to the island at this time was not coincidence, but fate.

As she listened, Evelyn's initial grogginess dissipated, and she became aware of her unfriendly response upon waking up.

"I'm sorry. I didn't mean to snap at you."

"It's alright," Adrian reassured her. "Do you think you can leave the room today?"

Evelyn took a deep breath and nodded as she got out of bed and made her way to the bathroom for a shower. Afterwards, Adrian assisted her with dressing, making sure she was stable on her feet. Once ready, they left the room together, with Adrian offering his arm to lean on.

They walked down the hotel corridor to meet Maruf in the outdoor patio area where he and Adrian sat the night before. As they approached him, he rose from his seat to greet Evelyn, his hand extended towards her in a welcome gesture, but Evelyn flinched.

"Get your hands out of my face!" she screamed. Shocked by her own reaction, Evelyn flushed with embarrassment. She turned away and buried her face in Adrian's shirt, mumbling an apology. Maruf remained composed, his expression kind and empathetic.

"It's okay, Evelyn," he said. "Adrian and I have faced many challenges together. You have not offended me, and we only wish to see you better."

Evelyn turned back toward him. "Adrian has told me a lot about you."

"After tonight's ritual, I think we'll know each other quite well," he smiled. "It will be at a secluded beach that I will take you to after the sun sets. I must leave now to prepare, but I promise to meet you both back here later."

After saying this, he turned and walked away, heading back through the clubhouse to the outside. Left alone, Adrian and Evelyn spent most of the day relaxing on the terrace of their hotel, admiring the deep blue waters in the distance. With Evelyn still weak, Adrian ordered a selection of fresh fruits and vegetables to help her regain some strength. Later in the morning, they shifted to a more relaxed spot on lawn chairs. Adrian carefully positioned an umbrella to provide Evelyn with ample shade, allowing her to enjoy the ocean view comfortably without the harsh sun.

"What do you think Maruf will show us tonight?" she asked.

"With him, it's best not to guess. But I trust him."

From their chase lounges, Adrian and Evelyn watched the progression of the sun across the clear morning sky. Evelyn, still recuperating, gazed longingly at the vibrant shore, yearning to partake in the activities she had imagined. As midday approached, they decided to retreat to their room for a bit of rest and a change of scenery. Inside, Adrian shared stories about past adventures to keep Evelyn's spirits up.

The sun was still shining over the Canary Islands at 6:30 PM when Maruf arrived to pick them up. He was dressed in a traditional white Nubian galabeya, a sight that Adrian was accustomed to from their time together in Egypt. Accompanying Maruf was a young man from the island who carried himself with a quiet and respectful demeanor.

Together, the group proceeded to the parking area. Maruf took the driver's seat of the Jeep, while Adrian assisted Evelyn into the back seat, making sure she was comfortable before sitting next to her. The young man from the island climbed into the passenger seat, adjusting it forward to give them more space in the back.

Their route followed a winding coastal road, flanked by towering cliffs on one side and expansive views of the sparkling ocean on the other. The scenic drive culminated at a secluded beach where the cliffs transitioned to soft sand. Maruf expertly maneuvered the Jeep onto the beach, parking in a spot that seemed isolated from the rest of the world.

The young assistant, who had remained silent throughout the journey, opened the trunk and pulled out a large, bulky bag that was nearly as tall as he was and hoisted it over his shoulder. Adrian steadied Evelyn as they navigated the mixed terrain of the beach, with its patches of sandy stretches interspersed with rocky outcroppings. Maruf took the lead, his eyes carefully surveying the area until he identified a particular spot.

"This is where we will perform the ritual," Maruf said, pointing to a flat area on the shore where the dark, volcanic sand met the rocky base of the cliffs.

The cliffs provided a natural cover, along with the tamarisk trees dotting the dark, volcanic terrain. The young man set the large bag down and began pulling out cushions, deftly arranging them to form an Arabic-style seating area nestled within one of the alcoves. With the seating in place, he turned his attention to the beach, gathering smooth, volcanic rocks to construct a fire pit. He carefully placed them in a circle on the dark sand, just in front of the seating area.

Once he had the fire pit arranged, he went off in search of wood, leaving Maruf, Adrian, and Evelyn to settle into the newly created space. They sank into the soft cushions, leaning comfortably against a rugged outcrop of rock that formed the backrest of their seating. As they relaxed, the sun began its descent into the ocean, casting a spectrum of colors across the horizon before sinking into the water.

Night quickly came upon them, with the stars twinkling in the sky above. Once his tasks were complete, the young man retreated to a nearby boulder by the water's edge, giving Maruf the space and privacy he needed for the night's events.

"What will we be doing here tonight?" Adrian asked.

"The ritual has two parts, and you know the first one because we did it in Egypt together before."

Maruf arranged the wood that the young man had gathered, setting up the fire pit for the ritual. From his satchel, he pulled out dried sagebrush, carefully placing the brittle leaves atop the pyramid of wood. Next, Maruf produced a shiny black stick from his pocket—a rare resin known for its potent spiritual properties, something Adrian had seen once before. He crumbled the resin over the wood and sage, preparing it for ignition and then struck a match.

He ignited the bottom of the pile, sending sparks flying as the sage and resin caught fire. The wood quickly crackled and burned, filling the air with a warm orange light and the fragrant scents of sage and burning wood. Maruf continued to add more sage and sprinkle in additional resin, intensifying the fire.

"What's that for?" Evelyn asked.

"These open the senses and will allow us to see the past." Maruf took a step back, giving the fire space as it burned higher. "Keep your eyes on the flames," he instructed. "Join me when you're ready."

Adrian and Evelyn watched in silence. The sparks from the fire shot up, stark against the dark night sky. Maruf began to chant in Arabic, his voice echoing powerfully over the sound of the ocean.

"Ya mawtā, kashfū al-māḍi! Ya mawtā, kashfū al-māḍi!"

Adrian and Evelyn joined in, repeating the incantation. Their voices merged, amplifying the power of the invocation.

"Ya mawtā, kashfū al-māḍi!"

The flames danced, revealing a vision. A city emerged, its design rippling outward like concentric circles on the surface of a pond. Around a stone temple, giants loomed—towering figures with ember-lit skin and braids thick as ropes, woven with the tales of eons. They marched toward the temple, their steps a drumbeat of ancient wars. Villagers clashed against the titans; desperation etched into their movements. At the center, two figures stood defiant—a man and a woman, their skin bronzed from the sun, their hair dark as the rich earth. They faced the onslaught, palms raised to the heavens.

"These are your past selves, who fought against the evil of the giants before the end of the world. Your ancient selves had special abilities and worked to close the portals that brought the giants to this world," Maruf said.

"Portals?" Adrian asked, looking into the flames.

Within the vision, their ancient forms stood, hands raised towards the heavens, amidst a circle of kin. These companions, their eyes alight with resolve and hands clutching primitive weapons, stood firm against the encroaching darkness. Around them, the villagers wore garments of simple woven fabric.

Evelyn's gaze was fixed on the flames as they swirled and leaped, drawing images of an ancient clash from the embers.

"Look," she whispered to Adrian, who stood beside her. "We're seeing ourselves."

Adrian nodded, his eyes wide open.

A giant appeared, larger and more imposing than the rest. His skin was like leather, and across his chest sprawled a scar in the shape of concentric circles, glowing with an ominous light that spoke of dark powers. His roar cut through the air, and his footsteps sent a shudder through the ground.

Then suddenly, the fire was blown out by a strong gust of cold wind, and Maruf's expression turned to one of deep concern.

"Come with me."

Maruf retrieved an ankh from his bag, an ancient Egyptian symbol of life that Adrian recognized immediately. Crafted from polished quartzite, it gleamed in the dim light. He gestured for them to follow him, leading the way to the shoreline. Feeling a bit uneasy, Evelyn leaned on Adrian for support as they walked towards the water.

Reaching the shoreline, Maruf continued walking, leading them into the ocean until the water reached his waist. Adrian and Evelyn followed closely, the cool water swirling around them as they positioned themselves around Maruf, ready for the ritual to begin.

"Your souls are bound to the past."

Maruf raised the giant ankh, allowing the moonlight to shine on it.

"Ya mawtā, kashfū al-māḍi!"

In the water's reflective surface, they saw glimpses of turbulent sea, a ship battled against the storm, creaking and groaning under the enormous pressure of the wind and waves. Onboard, figures were huddled together, their faces marked by determination to survive. Among them, were the man and woman, staring into the storm. Lightning flashed across the sky.

"We've seen this before…" Evelyn said. "Where are we going?"

"I don't know…" Adrian replied, looking to his friend.

"A long time ago, before the great flood, those who fought against the giants left Atlantis and sailed around the world to close the remaining portals. You were among them," Maruf replied.

The image in the water changed, revealing something that had been hidden from them until now.

In a frozen forest beside a lake, they raised their hands to the sky, caught in a desperate attempt to seal the portals above. Suddenly, a giant figure, twelve feet tall with concentric circles marked on his chest emerged holding a massive sword. He swung it and blood splattered against the white snow.

Evelyn screamed at the sight and let her weight fall into Adrian's arms. Emerging from the water, drenched and breathless, they stood with Maruf on the moonlit shore. The weight of their ancient memories hung heavily between them as Maruf, with a grave expression, delivered the inescapable truth.

"To stop the Masters, the portals must be sealed again, as history must repeat itself," Maruf said. "These ancient giants you fought against…they are the origin of the dark spirits you have faced back home."

Evelyn, still battling fever and now drenched, shivered uncontrollably.

"How are the Masters connected to giants?"

"They *were* the giants…" Maruf replied.

She looked at Adrian. "Did he kill us both?"

The vision didn't show if one of them had survived, but whatever happened was not good. He couldn't think of what to say.

"We're going to die, aren't we?" she said, continuing to shiver.

CHAPTER 10

AS THE FIRST rays of morning sun seeped through the curtains of their hotel room, Adrian and Evelyn stirred awake, still reeling from the ritual and its profound impact. The weight of Maruf's words and the intense visions they experienced lingered in their thoughts. They had embarked on a journey to uncover answers, but the truths they unearthed were more unsettling than they could have imagined.

"How are you?" Adrian asked.

Evelyn turned her head on the pillow to look at him, her face pale, her gestures weak.

"I don't want to die."

"We'll fight against it. No matter what."

Adrian reached out and pulled Evelyn close, holding her tightly, keenly aware that words alone could not ease her pain. Minutes passed in silence, broken only by the rhythm of their breathing. Eventually, Evelyn summoned the strength to lift herself up.

"Let's make the best out of being here," she said.

Like the day before, Adrian helped Evelyn out of bed and supported her as she shuffled into the bathroom for her shower. Afterwards, he assisted her with getting dressed, and once they were both ready, they left their hotel room. They moved slowly down the hotel corridor, Evelyn having grown accustomed to leaning on Adrian for support.

When they reached the lobby, they found Maruf waiting for them. His face wore an expression that mirrored the heaviness they both felt.

"How are you both feeling this morning?"

There was a brief silence as neither Adrian nor Evelyn responded.

Maruf then turned his attention directly to Evelyn. "How are you, my dear?"

She shook her head. "I don't feel well, and I'm not sure what to think about last night…but if we can, I'd love to see more of the island," she suggested.

Maruf and Adrian both understood that this was her way of mustering positivity in the face of despair.

"I can make that happen for you," Maruf smiled.

After they had something to eat, he led them back to the Wrangler and drove them to one of the islands' special beaches, known for its black sand and rugged lava formations. The sand was cool between their toes as they walked along the shore, with the waves gently lapping over their feet. Adrian supported Evelyn, helping her navigate as she took in the stunning surroundings.

As the sun climbed higher, Maruf took them to a quaint café. Shielded from the intensifying heat under a shaded patio, they enjoyed a meal of fresh seafood, followed by a selection of locally grown fruits. Later in the day, he led them to the botanical garden, filled with exotic plants and flowers. They wandered down the winding paths slowly, allowing Evelyn to see all that she could, without exacerbating her fatigue.

In the late afternoon, they settled on a secluded bench perched on a cliffside, where they watched the sky fill with streaks of fiery orange and pinks at sunset. Adrian wrapped his arm around Evelyn, creating a quiet moment of intimacy between them. Nearby, Maruf sat at a respectful distance, giving them space to cherish this time together.

Their day concluded with dinner on their hotel terrace, where Maruf ordered a spread of tapas and traditional Spanish dishes for them to enjoy. The night sea stretched out before them, with the starlit sky above. It was the day that Evelyn had wanted, but as the evening progressed, she grew more tired and somber.

"Can you take me back?" she whispered to Adrian.

Adrian assisted her to stand, and she turned to Maruf.

"Thank you for your hospitality… I'm really glad I got to meet you…"

In response, he gently took her hand. "It was an honor to meet you."

Adrian walked Evelyn back to their room. Once inside, he helped her change into more comfortable clothes and carefully assisted her into bed. As he adjusted the blankets around her, she saw the worry on his face.

"Would you like me to stay with you?" he asked.

Evelyn shook her head. "No, go spend the last few hours with your friend. We'll be together tomorrow."

Adrian kissed Evelyn on the forehead and quietly left the room. He returned to the lookout terrace, where Maruf was patiently waiting for him.

"She will feel better when you return home," Maruf said, seeing his friend approach. "That, you can be sure of."

"But what about what we saw yesterday? Are we going to have to sacrifice ourselves in this fight? Tell me I'm wrong, but I think we have to die to close the portals."

Maruf looked at Adrian with a serious face.

"Sometimes, we must confront the darkness within ourselves and our past. Your souls are tied to those portals…but I hold hope for you. Have faith in the love that binds you two together. Should you win this battle by paying with your lives…we both know that death is not the end."

Adrian struggled to take in Maruf's words. Familiar with the supernatural and having interacted with spirits, he understood that life extended beyond death in mysterious ways. However, the idea of sharing this harsh reality with Evelyn was unbearable—that their death was not just probable, but perhaps necessary.

"Thank you, Maruf, for everything," Adrian said, his voice filled with emotion. "I hope that someday, somehow, our spirits meet again."

"Never despair, my dear friend. Even in the face of darkness, there is light."

The two men stood and shared a tight hug. Then, Adrian broke away and left the terrace, walking down towards his cabin without looking back. Maruf stood watching him go with sadness in his heart. After Adrian disappeared from view, he turned to face the ocean, the cool breeze brushing against his face.

Inside the room, Adrian found Evelyn asleep but restless, her breathing uneven and her body shivering under the covers. He slid into bed beside her, wrapping his arms around her, offering warmth through the night. As he held her close, he thought about their journey home tomorrow and how something was now most certainly coming for them.

The next morning, Adrian quietly got out of bed to pack their belongings while Evelyn continued to sleep for an extra hour. Once everything was ready, Adrian carried their luggage to the lobby and asked the receptionist to call a taxi for their trip to the airport.

During the first leg of their flight, Evelyn felt extremely ill. She gripped a paper bag tightly, especially during bouts of turbulence, worried she might be sick. Her discomfort persisted throughout their layover in Lisbon, which felt endless. As they sat in the airport lounge, her fatigue and paleness blended into the dull, gray surroundings of the terminal.

The second flight was no less challenging at the start. The drone of the engines and the confined space did little to ease her discomfort. But as the plane neared Massachusetts, a subtle shift took place. Gradually, Evelyn straightened up from her slumped position in the seat. Over the last stretch, her complexion took on a healthier glow, and the brightness returned to her eyes.

As strange as it was, surprisingly, as the plane began its descent through the dark morning sky toward Logan Airport,

Evelyn found herself suddenly alert and sitting upright in her seat, looking out the window at the city lights flickering below.

A taxi drove them to Evelyn's apartment after they landed. When they arrived at 5 AM, the familiarity of her place brought a small sense of relief. Exhausted from travel, they took a brief shower together before collapsing into bed for a few hours of sleep. They were well aware that tomorrow would not be a day of rest but rather one filled with the challenges and revelations of their impending battle.

By noon, they were awake again, both seated at the kitchen table with coffee in hand. Evelyn, looking troubled, broke the silence.

"I'm not going to the office today."

The very idea of returning to work seemed ridiculous now, her mind increasingly unwilling to think about real estate.

Adrian was determined not to let his emotions control him, focused on the next thing to do.

"Please call Mayor Jenkins and tell him we're available to see him today. As we prepare for what may come, we'll want to know what he has to say," he said, attempting a smile and trying to inject a sliver of optimism into their situation.

After finishing their coffee, they quickly unpacked and got dressed. Evelyn reached into her purse, pulled out her cell phone, and made the call. The mayor's voice was tense when he answered on the third ring.

"Evelyn, where have you been? I've been trying to reach you."

Adrian stood nearby, listening intently to the conversation.

"We travelled out of state."

"But your phone was off..."

"We're back now and ready to meet with you," she said, refusing to explain herself.

After a pause, the mayor softened his tone. "I'm leaving work early today. Can you come to my house in two hours?"

"We'll be there," she replied, staring into Adrian's eyes.

Evelyn hung up the phone, and without saying a word, Adrian left the bedroom and went to the living room. She followed him and observed as he packed some of his strange belongings into his duffle bag, including a black clay cauldron from the closet, a bottle of rubbing alcohol, and his hunting knife. He appeared unfazed by the impending threat of death, and she knew Adrian was a soldier at heart, who would always take action rather than dwell on his fate.

Adrian initially dismissed Mayor Jenkins's request to check his home for paranormal activity as baseless fears. However, after their encounters with Maruf and discovering the ties between their past and the current excavations in Baneford, the mayor's plea now held more weight and urgency.

At the designated time, Evelyn and Adrian drove through town to Mayor Jenkins's residence. He seemed nervous as he greeted them at the front door. He hurriedly led them into the dining room, where he had previously met with Saul and Cavil.

"What do you need from me?" Adrian asked, looking at the mayor intently.

The directness caused the mayor to stumble over his words. "There's something I need to tell you… But first I want you to check my home…you know…to see if there are any evil spirits here."

"Let's begin," he said, preferring not to waste time.

"Yes…yes, please," the mayor responded with a hint of unease.

They left Evelyn alone, as they began walking through the house. Adrian led the way, with the mayor at his heels. As they entered the living room, the afternoon light streamed in through sheer curtains. Adrian stopped in the middle of the room, closed his eyes for a moment, then spread out his hands with his palms facing downwards. His fingers trembled slightly as he scanned the room. *Nothing.*

In the kitchen, Adrian walked around the large quartz island and opened cabinets but found no trace of anything out of the ordinary. Going up to the second floor, the old colonial staircase creaked beneath their feet. At the top, Adrian turned left into a study filled with bookshelves and an antique desk. He ran his fingers along the spines of the books, then stood still.

"I don't sense anything."

They went down the hallway, briefly stopping at each bedroom for Adrian to take a quick look. Finally, they reached the closed door of the master bedroom and Adrian turned to the mayor for approval before entering.

"My wife's not here…she went to stay with her parents. You can go in."

Adrian entered the bedroom, dimly lit by the glow of a bedside lamp. He took a moment to survey his surroundings, noting the elegant bedspread and faint scent of lavender. He moved further into the room, his fingers brushing against the mahogany dresser. He found nothing in its drawers or in the closet. He moved to the windows, peering out into the sunny afternoon. The curtains rustled gently in the breeze.

"The room is clear, Mayor. There are no signs of any dark energy or evil spirits in your home."

He swallowed hard in response, and they returned to the dining area, where Evelyn was waiting patiently. They settled in the seats next to her, and the mayor launched into a series of complaints about the town—zoning issues, problems with the water and sewer department, and his struggle to find a new assistant. It was a stream of nervous babble that was clearly not what he'd wished to talk about.

"What aren't you telling us?" Adrian interjected.

The color drained from Mayor Jenkins's face. "There's something I have to tell you about. Someone, actually…"

"Who?"

"His name is Saul Griesmeyer… He's a businessman who's been buying up land near the Dyeworks factory. He knew Ursula, and he was here, sitting right in that chair," he said, pointing to the seat occupied by Evelyn.

"Why did you allow property sales to someone linked with Ursula and the Masters?" Evelyn asked, narrowing her eyes at him.

Beads of sweat formed on his forehead, and he shifted uncomfortably in his chair.

"What have you done?" Adrian demanded, banging his fist on the table.

"He came here demanding that I sell him the factory…he said he would kill me. I signed the offer…but the deal can't go through until I get signatures…that's buys us some time…he's also involved with the excavations at Echo Lake somehow."

"He worked for Ursula?" Evelyn asked.

"I think it might be the other way around—that she worked for him."

Evelyn and Adrian shared a glance, contemplating the potential threat this man posed, now illuminated by the mayor's evident fear.

Adrian stood, taking off his jacket and tossing it onto the table.

"Be quiet and be still."

Adrian reached out, clasping Mayor Jenkins's hands firmly in his own. Evelyn watched as Adrian's features eased into a calm, almost trance-like state. After a tense moment, he released the mayor's hands.

"They plan to summon the Masters."

The mayor leaned back in his chair and looked out the window. "Can you stop it?"

"I will," Adrian replied.

Mayor Jenkins looked at him and then shook his head. "I know this town is cursed... It always was..."

Adrian, showing little interest in hearing more, subtly nodded to Evelyn. Understanding his gesture, she quickly got to her feet, and they both headed towards the front door, leaving the mayor alone with his worries. Outside, the daylight was beginning to fade.

They walked to their car, with Adrian taking the passenger seat and Evelyn sliding behind the wheel. She turned the key in the ignition, and as the car pulled away from the mayor's residence, Adrian turned to Evelyn, a serious look on his face.

"There's something I need to see for myself... Please, take us to Echo Lake."

Evelyn followed the route that cut through town before turning onto Pennyworth Road, which gradually increased in elevation. As they reached the top of the hill, they could see the lake spread out below them, its surface a mirror under the impending night sky. They continued down the hill to the parking area. In contrast to when they had come to see the excavations, there were few cars there now.

Evelyn and Adrian got out of the car and walked down to the shore, where the spring dew had dampened the grassy banks right up to the water's edge. They stood there for a moment, remembering the battle from only a few months ago. Then he guided her to a secluded spot nestled between the trees.

He reached into his duffel bag and retrieved his clay cauldron. He poured alcohol into it and then struck a match. It caught instantly, casting an orange glow on their faces. They both leaned in and focused on the flames, and a vision slowly began to materialize within the flickering light.

In the icy woods, a man and woman meditated. Dark hair fell to their shoulders, tan skin aglow in the firelight. serene under the moon. Palms upturned, reaching for the starry sky. Suddenly, a giant appears. He bears the concentric circle symbol on his chest. The woman stood up and ran, but the man stayed.

Adrian knew that he was looking at his past self. Evelyn felt her heart begin to race.

The giant carried a sword of immense size and swung it forcefully, cutting the man in two. Blood sprayed everywhere.

As the vision faded, Evelyn's scream cut through the night.

"This is where I died..." Adrian said, as he lay down on the ground, speaking softly. "I can feel it in my body now..."

"What about me?" Evelyn said.

The woman she believed to be herself was not there.

"We crossed the ocean with our people to close the portals. I came here...you went to...Dyeworks...or whatever it used to be."

Immediately, Evelyn stood up.

"Did I die there? I want to know. Let's go there now," she insisted.

"I can't tonight, I'm not strong enough" Adrian said, barely sitting up straight. "Please, let me recover tonight."

This time it was Evelyn who helped Adrian stand and get back to the car, as the ritual had drained him, with the visceral memory of being slain making its way through his body. That night, she put him in bed early letting him recover, and went back out of the living room to think.

Was I killed with him, or did in happen at Dyeworks? Evelyn wondered. *Why did I leave him?* Unlike what they'd concluded from the visions with Maruf, it now seemed that they had not died together, but apart.

CHAPTER 11

EVELYN WAS UP early the next day, on her laptop, busy tracking the property acquisitions around the Dyeworks tannery that the mayor had mentioned. She searched through property records, following a tangled web of LLCs acquiring properties near the Dyeworks tannery. After hours of searching, she came across the name mentioned by the mayor—Saul Griesmeyer. As she dug further, she discovered that he wasn't just a businessman, but a ruthless opportunist, preying on struggling towns like Baneford. His reputation was tainted with a string of ruined communities in pursuit of personal gain.

Adrian woke up slowly and remained in bed for a few more hours. Around noon, he walked by the office, looking more like himself.

"Come look at this," Evelyn said, waving him over.

He approached her desk, leaning in over her shoulder. She had pulled up a map on her laptop screen highlighting the properties Saul Griesmeyer had acquired around the Dyeworks area. They were positioned around the site from every direction.

"He's going to get access to the tunnels, whether the mayor sells or not," Adrian said.

Evelyn clicked on the next tab, where there was a news article about the strange environmental contamination that had affected Saverill, a small-town northwest of Baneford, causing some residents to go permanently insane.

"That's what happens when he comes…"

"Not contamination….a curse," Adrian corrected. "We need to be careful when we head to Dyeworks this evening. We need to make sure that you are connected to the portal there, as I was connected to the one at the lake."

"And if he has people there?" Evelyn asked.

"I will kill them."

He said the words with a sense of finality, but it was very unlike the man Evelyn had first met, who had opposed killing under all circumstances.

"You don't know anything about him…"

"Then help by learning as much as you can while I get ready for tonight."

Adrian left her in the office and made his way to the living room. He grabbed his duffle bag and started packing for their mission later that night. The goal was clear—confirm that Evelyn was connected to the portal at Dyeworks, just as he was connected to the one at Echo Lake.

Meanwhile, Evelyn began reaching out to property owners in the vicinity of Dyeworks, extending her inquiries a few blocks outwards. With each call, she probed whether they had been contacted by Saul or received any recent offers on their properties. The responses varied, with some oblivious to the situation, others didn't respond, and a few seemed wary, hinting at knowledge they were reluctant to share. However, the most alarming conversation was with Mr. Moulton Jr. Knowing his father her entire life made it particularly harrowing to learn that Saul, along with an associate, had forcibly coerced him into selling his property through assault and threats. Disturbed by these revelations, Evelyn shared the details of Moulton Jr.'s distressing encounter with Adrian as soon as she ended the call.

They decided to wait until sunset to leave the apartment, because, as Adrian said, the veil between this world and the next was thinnest at dusk. When they stepped out, the diminishing light was already casting shadows on the ground. They got into the car and headed towards Dyeworks, passing Evelyn's office on the way and then proceeding all the way down Main Street to the industrial quarter.

Evelyn parked a few blocks away, and they walked down the street, scanning their surroundings for any signs of suspicious activity. The streets were eerily empty, except for the homeless individuals lingering in the alleyways, keeping their distance. As they approached the construction fence, they could make out the chaotic debris of the old factory beyond it—piles of concrete, cement, and twisted metal scattered everywhere.

Adrian motioned for Evelyn to follow as he led her towards a section of the fence, partially obscured by a towering maple tree. From his bag, Adrian produced a pair of wire cutters and carefully snipped away at the chain-link fence. He then forcefully pushed back a section to make room for their entrance.

From their position in the center of the lot, they were shielded from the street by the partial walls still standing and the construction fence in the distance. Adrian led Evelyn to a large concrete slab, angled and resting on other debris, where he gestured for her to sit. She brushed off some dust and small rocks before settling down. He placed a clay cauldron on the ground a few feet away and poured in alcohol. Checking his pockets and coming up empty, he asked her to toss him the matches from his duffle bag. As Evelyn stood back up to retrieve them, her foot caught on a rock, causing her ankle to twist. She lost her balance and fell, scraping her thigh on a jagged piece of metal rebar protruding from the ground.

"Ouch!" she screamed.

He rushed over and helped her back up, noticing the blood seeping through her jeans. It was a serious cut. He quickly retrieved the hunting knife from his bag and cut away the fabric to assess the wound. As he inspected it, drops of blood fell from her knee to the ground. Suddenly, the earth beneath them trembled. The shaking intensified, sending a low rumble through the rubble around them.

Evelyn tensed, her voice barely a whisper. "What was that?"

Adrian tensed his jaw, his eyes cold and distant. "Let's leave and get you cleaned up."

"But what about the ritual? I'm okay…" she said, determined to continue with their plan.

She took a few steps to show him that she was fine, but Adrian proceeded to gather the cauldron, placing it back into his bag.

"You felt the tremors. The earth itself reacted to your blood…its confirmed…you died here…and there's something else… For us to close the portals, we'll have to use our blood."

Evelyn was acutely aware of Adrian's aversion to blood magic, making his mention of it particularly significant. With a shared understanding, they silently left the ruins of the Dyeworks site, navigating carefully through the scattered rubble. Evelyn winced with each step, her shoes crunching on the gravel. After squeezing through a narrow gap in the fence, they crossed the street to where their car was parked. In the background, they could hear the faint sounds of homeless people moving through the spaces between abandoned factories.

The ride back to Evelyn's apartment on Mox Street was tense, filled with uneasy silence. Once inside, Adrian wasted no time retrieving the first-aid kit. He knelt beside her in the living room and began tending to her wound. He peeled back the cloth covering it.

"This needs cleaning, and it might sting a bit," he warned.

He carefully dabbed at the cut with a gauze pad, and Evelyn braced for it. As Adrian was finishing securing the bandage, the moment was shattered by the crash of the front door slamming open, sending shockwaves through the apartment.

The sound of approaching footsteps grew louder until two distinct figures appeared in the doorway. One was an older man in a suit with graying hair at his temples. His eyes scanned the room with a sharp intensity. Standing next to him was a large man with broad shoulders, taller and broader than Adrian and radiating a sense of aggression. It was clear he was ready to cause harm if given the opportunity.

"Go!" Adrian's voice rang out, urging Evelyn to escape through the window.

However, she remained frozen in place, her eyes locked onto Saul and Cavil as they stood ominously at the entrance of her living room.

Trapped with no clear path to escape, Adrian made a split-second decision and charged at Cavil, their bodies crashing into a side table and knocking over a lamp. The ceramic base shattered into countless pieces on the floor as they grappled with each other, clawing and throwing punches. Adrian landed a powerful blow to Cavil's jaw, causing him to recoil momentarily before responding with a strike to Adrian's ribcage, making him grunt in pain.

They broke apart and got to their feet, continuing the fight in the tight space. They exchanged punches, the sound of their heavy breathing mixing with the thuds of fists hitting flesh. Cavil then pushed Adrian against a bookcase, causing family photos to tumble down and frames to break, scattering glass across the floor. He grabbed one of the wooden chairs and flung it towards Adrian, who narrowly avoided getting hit as it smashed against the wall.

Cavil threw a barrage of punches at Adrian's face, but Adrian skillfully avoided them and countered with his own, landing two hard blows. Seeing an opening, he grabbed Cavil by the hair and slammed his head against the wall, and then grabbed Cavil's arm and yanked him forcefully out of the living room into the hallway. Meanwhile, in the living room, Saul kept his focus on Evelyn as she watched them fight.

Before Cavil could regain his footing, Adrian landed a powerful kick to his gut, sending him staggering into the kitchen. He crashed against the fridge with a resounding bang. As Adrian scanned for a weapon, his eyes landed on a plate on the counter. He snatched it and smashed it over Cavil's head. The assault left Cavil dazed, a trickle of blood running down from a gash on his forehead. Wasting no time, Adrian pulled his arm back and delivered a hard right hook to Cavil's face. It sent Cavil reeling back onto the kitchen counter, where he finally slumped to the ground, knocked out cold.

Adrian quickly returned to the living room, calling out to Evelyn.

"Now!" he shouted.

Evelyn rushed past Saul at the door, bumping him with her shoulder. The force pushed him against the door frame, and he immediately began coughing violently, bringing a red-stained handkerchief to his mouth. Without pausing, Evelyn and Adrian dashed for the front door, leaving Saul coughing and scowling in the doorway. Evelyn snatched her keys and purse as they burst out of the apartment and raced toward her car.

Adrian, with bruises on his face from the altercation, sat in the driver's seat and gripped the steering wheel tightly. Evelyn, sitting beside him, scanned the road ahead and the rearview mirror for any signs of being followed.

"Where are we going, Adrian?" she asked.

"The only place here that I know," he replied.

"Those men...that must be Saul Griesmeyer."

Adrian pulled into the gravel driveway of the Riverside Inn, nestled on the banks of the river. The sight of the old building stirred memories, because it was here that Evelyn had first found

Adrian seeking refuge upon his arrival in Baneford. The inn, once a grand colonial mansion, remained as weathered and worn as it was on their last visit. They parked across the street and quickly made their way inside.

The wooden door groaned loudly as they entered. Everything looked old and faded. At the center stood an impressive grand staircase. The musty smell of mildew hung heavily in the air. Fluorescent bulbs buzzed and flickered above the check-in desk, where an older gentleman sat, clearly caught off guard by the unexpected walk-in. Evelyn quickly approached, while Adrian stood a few feet back.

"We need a room for the night, please."

The clerk's eyes shifted past Evelyn to take in Adrian's disheveled appearance. He observed the bruises, bloodstain on his face, and torn clothes, suggesting he had been in some kind of altercation. Despite his curiosity, the man maintained a professional demeanor and simply nodded before pushing the registration book towards Evelyn.

"Of course," he replied politely while trying not to stare. "May I see some identification, please?"

Evelyn promptly handed over her own ID.

"Just mine will be fine," she said firmly.

Sensing the urgency in Evelyn's voice, the clerk quickly scanned her ID, deciding not to ask for Adrian's. He returned her identification and handed her the key to room 202. Evelyn took it and joined Adrian at the staircase, both eager to retreat to the privacy of their room. They ascended the grand staircase to the second floor, making their way down the corridor to a room at the far end.

The room was small and somewhat worn, but it possessed a quaint charm, offering a view of the Washisund River lined with the skeletal remains of Baneford's old factories; stark reminders of the town's bustling industrial heyday. With the door shut behind them, Adrian turned to Evelyn.

"The fight came faster than we expected..."

"Are you okay?" Evelyn asked, looking at the cut under Adrian's eye and the scrapes marking his skin.

"I'm fine," he said, stepping into the bathroom.

He removed his shirt and began tending to his wounds with a damp towel. His knuckles were already starting to bruise, and there were scratches scattered across his body, some old scars from past fights mixed in with the new ones. Evelyn sat on the corner of the bed, staring at them.

"He knows where I live."

Adrian tossed the wet towel in his hand into the sink and stepped out of the bathroom.

"He wanted us because he intends to release the Masters..."

"The souls of evil giants," Evelyn laughed, trying to make light of what they'd learned.

Adrian sat down at the edge of the bed next to Evelyn, their knees touching. He brushed a stray lock of hair behind her ear, and she pressed her body into his, bringing her face closer.

"We can survive this," he said, attempting to impart some hope.

He leaned back, pulling her down with him, their lips meeting in a passionate kiss. Evelyn's hands traced down his chest, enjoying the warmth of his skin. She fumbled with the button of his jeans, then slid them off. She removed her top, and Adrian's lips left a trail of kisses from her neck down to her collarbone. Evelyn tangled her fingers in his hair, pulling him closer, yearning for the weight of his body against hers. The bed creaked under them as they moved together. Their bodies edged closer, and then together, they reached climax, waves of pleasure overtaking them.

They laid in bed together afterwards in silence. All that remained was to endure the night together. Evelyn turned off the lamp and thought of ways they could possibly win this battle. Adrian had always held a deep disdain for blood magic and those who practiced, but perhaps giving into the darkness just once was the right thing to do.

CHAPTER 12

BREAKFAST WAS TERRIBLE at the Riverside Inn. Nothing more than weak, bitter coffee, eggs, and toast with jam in little plastic containers. Sitting across from each other at the table, Adrian and Evelyn shared a heavy silence, the unsettling events from the previous night lingering in their minds. They knew that confrontations were inevitable now.

"We're going to need to go back to Dyeworks and Echo Lake today," Adrian said, his voice low but urgent.

Evelyn nodded slowly, her eyes tracing the patterns on the coffee cup. "They're going to be waiting for us… What's our plan?"

"You should call Casey. We need somewhere to hide, and we're going to need some help," he suggested, his brow furrowed in thought.

Evelyn took a deep breath and reached for her phone. She dialed Casey's number and waited, feeling the weight of each ring.

"Hello?" Casey answered, a slight hint of worry in her voice.

"It's me… Something bad happened last night," Evelyn said, wasting no time.

Casey fell silent on the other end of the phone, her breath held before releasing a heavy sigh. "Are you okay?"

"We're okay... But we need somewhere to hide until we figure out what we're gonna do and we can't go back to my place."

"Why?"

"Because that's where they came for us."

Evelyn explained how two intruders had burst into their apartment the night before and shared what the mayor had told them about Saul Griesmeyer and his interest in Dyeworks.

"Can we hide with you?" she asked finally.

Despite her fear, Casey's response was immediate. "Of course. Come over right away."

Evelyn ended the call and turned to face Adrian.

"We can go there."

They gathered their belongings and quickly left the room at the Riverside Inn, making their way down the dimly lit hallway and descending the grand staircase to the lobby. They could see their car parked across the street, with the river glistening behind it. As they headed towards their vehicle, Adrian and Evelyn heard a distant rumble getting closer.

Before they could turn around, a van screeched to a halt beside them. Cavil leaped out, taser in hand, charging towards them. Adrian tried to grab the weapon, but Cavil dodged, jabbing the taser into Adrian's chest, sending him crumpling to the ground. Simultaneously, Evelyn turned to run, but Cavil was quick on her heels. He caught up to her and thrust the taser into her back. The shock sent her body seizing up, and she fell to the pavement.

With no one around to witness, Cavil swiftly zip-tied their hands behind their backs and dragged them into the van. Inside, Saul sat behind the wheel, his grin malicious as Cavil secured duct tape over their mouths. With Adrian and Evelyn incapacitated, the engine started again, and the van rolled forward. They lay on the van's floor, unable to see out as they were driven for about ten minutes.

When the van stopped, and Cavil opened the door, they were on the industrial side of Main Street, near the old Dyeworks factory. Cavil dragged them out and into a deserted retail store with boarded-up windows. Inside, Evelyn noticed the address, realizing they were in one of the properties recently acquired by Saul.

Cavil pushed Adrian and Evelyn into chairs at a weathered table in the center of the abandoned store. As he moved, the sound of crumbling drywall crackled under his boots. He yanked the duct tape from their mouths and then circled the table to sit beside Saul, directly across from Adrian and Evelyn. Saul fixed his gaze on Evelyn, leaning forward with an intense stare.

"Evelyn," he said ominously, speaking only to her. "You don't know what you're up against. You're destined to lose this fight."

His words felt like an inescapable promise. Saul's eyes gleamed with satisfaction as he saw the fear in hers. He unveiled Ursula's knife from under his suit jacket. It was the same one with the handle made of bone that Evelyn used to defeat Ursula. She thought it had been destroyed in the explosion.

"Who are you?" Adrian demanded.

Cavil's muscles tightened at the aggressive tone aimed at his boss, but Saul signaled for him to stay composed.

"I am the one who will complete what Ursula started…me and my special friend, whom you'll soon meet."

Adrian's anger rose as Saul set Ursula's knife on the table.

Evelyn's eyes fixated on the knife, whispering promises of an escape.

"The last time you touched this knife, you were allowed to live," Saul continued. "The Masters gave you what you wanted. That's what I'm going to ask of you…to use this knife again in sacrifice…or you can die."

Though she knew he represented everything they were fighting against, she couldn't stop herself from considering Saul's offer. The last time she held that knife, she had rescued Adrian and herself from certain death. *Maybe there's another way.*

"We can't let them win," Adrian said to her, his heart aching, watching her teeter at the edge of darkness.

Before Evelyn could respond, the sound of approaching footsteps echoed in the back stairwell. Moments later, the rear egress door creaked open, and Slater stepped into the room. Adrian and Evelyn shared a moment of confusion, attempting to recall where they had encountered him before. Then, it came—he was the archaeologist Evelyn had conversed with in the woods, who now appeared to have some connection to Saul and the Masters.

"We've stumbled upon new skeletal remains, and there are underground passages beneath the massive stones—extending far down," he announced to Saul and Cavil.

"It must bring back familiar feelings for you," Saul replied.

"I see you have them."

As Slater circled the table, he flashed a grin that Adrian and Evelyn found unsettlingly familiar. They noticed a significant detail on Cavil's hand—a ring adorned with concentric circles raised on its surface, identical to the symbol they had seen in their visions, branded on the chest of the giant who had killed them. Wondering how this scientist could possibly be linked to those ancient beings, Adrian subtly began to work the zip tie binding his hands, striving to free himself without letting them notice.

"Do you remember me?" Slater said, speaking to Evelyn. Twelve thousand years ago, you thought you escaped me." His hand came down on the table hard, making a loud thud. "You didn't," he smiled.

Discretely rubbing the zip tie against the sharp corner of his chair, Adrian felt it slowly breaking apart. As the plastic gave way, he brought his hands forward and catapulted himself towards Slater, aiming to take him down. But with an unexpected display of strength from the older academic, Slater effortlessly grabbed Adrian by the throat, yanking him out of the air and hoisting him off the ground like a rag doll.

"No!" Evelyn screamed.

Adrian struggled violently, trying to break free, while Cavil and Saul burst into laughter. Saul's laughter quickly turned into a fit of violent coughing, and he pulled out a handkerchief to spit blood into it. Slater flashed another wicked grin at Evelyn. Then he delivered a brutal blow with the side of his fist to Adrian's head, knocking him out cold, letting his limp body drop to the floor.

Evelyn continued to scream until Cavil silenced her by placing a strip of duct tape back firmly across her mouth. Then he lifted her up from the chair, and with Slater and Saul at either side, they left the retail store, leaving Adrian unconscious on the ground.

***

Adrian lay on the hard floor, unconscious for several minutes. Gradually, he stirred, his eyes fluttering open with a gasp of breath as he came to. As consciousness crawled back, the chill of the floor seeped into his bones. Surveying his surroundings, he found himself alone in the deserted store, the silence amplifying his panic. *Evelyn was gone.*

Pushing himself to his knees, he remembered their plan to go to Casey's apartment. Fumbling with his phone, he quickly dialed Casey's number, the only other number he knew besides Evelyn's. After a few rings, she picked up.

"Casey, it's Adrian. Something bad has happened. Evelyn's been taken."

There was a moment of silence as she processed the information.

"Taken by who? Are you okay?"

"There's no time to explain… I need your help to get her back… Can you pick me up. I'm near Dyeworks?"

"Yeah. I'm on my way."

When Casey pulled up, her eyes were wide with concern. Adrian climbed into the SUV and filled her in on the way to her apartment. He told her about Saul, the archeologist, the portals and their connection to the Masters, who were once the ancient giants being excavated.

"Can you save her?"

Adrian gave a subtle nod, but deep down, he knew it wasn't just her body they were trying to save now, but her soul.

"It depends…"

"What's happened to her? Depends on what?" Casey interrupted.

"They're going to try to tempt her to make a sacrifice to the Masters again. If she gives in, I don't know what will happen."

Casey parked the car in front of her building.

"Why her?" Casey asked, as they approached her door. She unlocked it and let Adrian in.

Adrian turned and stared directly into Casey's blue eyes, hoping that the unbelievable words he had to say would somehow make sense to her.

"Because thousands of years ago, living different lives, Evelyn and I fought against the giants…and we died to banish them from the earth. Our souls are linked to his town…and to them."

Casey slowly sat down on her couch. There was nothing she could say in response because she knew, deep in her heart, that Adrian was not crazy. She'd seen too much with him and Evelyn to doubt him now.

"What do you plan to do?"

"We have to save her…but first I have to close the portal at Echo Lake. That way, there's only one remaining."

"What if you can't?"

It was a reasonable question, but one that required Adrian to share the full truth.

"Dying would be better than Evelyn giving her soul to the Masters for eternity."

Casey's face crumpled, her voice breaking as she absorbed the full weight of his words. "That's Evelyn we're talking about—how can you even think about letting her die?"

"There's always hope," Adrian offered.

Casey sobbed, her emotions overwhelming her. She wiped her tears, struggling with the reality of losing her best friend.

"She doesn't deserve this. It's not fair…"

"No…but I will need your help."

He understood the enormity of what he was asking: for her to come to terms with her best friend's death, to risk her own life, and to trust him with matters that seemed completely out of his control.

"What do we need to do?"

Adrian smiled at her, showing appreciation for her strength and resolve.

"A ritual at Echo Lake… And I'll need a few things… Do you have any weapons?"

Casey hesitated for a moment before her eyes shifted to the coat closet by the door. She went to it and retrieved a steel pipe from inside and brought it back to him.

"It's been there a while…" she said. Then she opened the coffee table drawer and pulled out brass knuckles. "And there's this."

He took the pipe from her and slipped the brass knuckles on, trying them on for size.

"There are a few more things that I will need—a bag to carry things, candles and a lighter, a mason jar, and a sharp knife."

Casey took a deep breath and nodded before standing up to collect the items that Adrian had requested. She spent a few minutes walking back and forth in the apartment before returning to the dining room. She laid everything out on the table in front of him and began packing it all into the bag.

"What time are we heading out?"

"As soon as the sun begins to set."

Acknowledging the plan, Casey excused herself to her bedroom, needing a moment alone. The weight of the evening ahead pressed down on her, and once in her room, she sank to the floor, taking deep breaths to gather her courage.

After some time had passed, she emerged from the room, determined to do everything in her power to save her friend. She knew that Adrian wouldn't have shared the harsh reality with her unless he truly believed it, as he remained willing, as always, to sacrifice himself for Evelyn.

When she returned, she looked at him with a mix of gratitude and fear in her eyes.

"What if we all die tonight?"

"Something tells me that won't be your fate, and hopefully not ours either…"

When day light had faded into a cool spring evening, Casey and Adrian drove east across town towards the lake. Before long, they were on the winding road that climbed to a vantage point, offering a panoramic view of Echo Lake from above. Descending the other side, she guided the car into the parking area, now sparsely populated with just a few cars.

They exited the SUV into the cool night air, quietly making their way through the woods toward the lake. From afar, the faint sounds of activity at the excavation site on the hill were audible, indicating that work was still ongoing. As they drew nearer to the lake, the noises from the hill gradually receded into the background. Adrian finally stopped at the water's edge.

"That's where we drowned Hendrick," Adrian said, pointing ahead of him.

"I know," Casey said, her voice steady, catching Adrian off guard. "After what he did to me, I had Evelyn take me here. I needed to see it for myself."

Adrian gestured subtly towards the woods.

"Let's find a more private spot."

They retreated to the edge of the woods and slipped behind a veil of trees, walking about thirty feet into a secluded enclave shrouded by thick bushes and overgrown vegetation. As the forest canopy obscured the moonlight, the air thickened with an ancient, expectant silence.

Adrian knelt on the ground and opened his duffle bag as Casey knelt beside him. He pulled out a mason jar and a handful of candles, placing them in a circle around them. He lit the candles, then began to pack the jar with soil, digging with his hands.

"What are you doing?" Casey whispered.

"My blood must merge with the earth, reconnecting with the energies it once knew," Adrian explained.

He sliced a small cut across his palm, and droplets of his blood dripped into the jar, darkening the dirt. Clearing his throat, Adrian began to chant the words Maruf had taught him.

"Ya mawtā, kashfū al-māḍi!"

His voice grew louder, more forceful with each repetition. As he chanted, the air around them began to vibrate, the ground beneath them thrumming with a deep, resonant energy. Suddenly, the sky above cracked open with a brilliant flash, illuminating the forest like daylight. The ground shook, and the energy around them intensified, swirling with visible currents of air that whipped through the trees, rustling leaves.

"Ya mawtā, kashfū al-māḍi!" Adrian's voice echoed through the forest.

The pulsing energy around them peaked, then, as abruptly as it had escalated, it stopped. The candles snuffed out simultaneously and profound silence enveloped them. Casey and Adrian felt the air shift, a subtle release as if a great breath had been exhaled.

"What do you feel?" Casey asked.

"This portal is almost closed," Adrian replied. "But they can still use Evelyn to open it again...along with the other portal at Dyeworks. We need to go there, now."

CHAPTER 13

SAUL DROVE THE van away from the abandoned retail store, with Evelyn sitting in the back between Cavil and Slater. Her heart raced as they made their way through town, heading straight towards the Dyeworks. But instead of stopping there, they continued past it and pulled up in front of a residential brick building that looked like her own.

The building looked abandoned, yet they forcefully ushered her from the van and through its entrance. She guessed this was another recent acquisition of Saul's near the factory. They led her down a dark corridor on the ground floor and into a bleak, rundown apartment. The room was stark and unwelcoming, with broken windows and glass shards littering the floor. In the center, a single metal chair sat beneath a solitary lightbulb dangling from the ceiling.

Cavil shoved Evelyn into the chair under the stark light and swiftly ripped the duct tape from her mouth. He then fastened her already zip-tied hands to the chair, securing her in place. Isolated on one side of the room, Evelyn faced Cavil and Saul, who leaned against the wall a few yards away. Slater remained standing in front of her, towering over her.

"Listen closely, Evelyn," Slater said, leaning in. "We can handle this the easy way or the hard way, but there's only one way you survive. Tonight, Orion's belt aligns perfectly above

Baneford, just as it did 12,000 years ago. You're going to help me reopen the portals so my people can return to Earth."

"What are you?" Evelyn asked, unable to understand this man's connection to all of this.

Slater smiled, staring directly into her eyes.

"We were descendants of the Anunnaki, worshipped in Sumeria as gods for thousands of years. We came from the stars, through interdimensional portals, to rule over this Earth. We were the ones who taught humans to build temples and create civilizations. We taught you astronomy and agriculture, lifting you from ignorance. But you were always meant to be our slaves."

"You look human to me."

"This curse," Slater said, gesturing at his own body. "When humans tried to close the portals, it caused a great flood. Those of us who were practicing the dark arts were cast into the shadows, becoming what you now call the Masters. Others, like me, suffered a fate far worse. We have reincarnated among you, as humans, embodying our humiliation."

She could see the disgust he held for her, but also for his own body.

"You're not a god," Evelyn sneered.

Saul and Cavil observed the exchange, silent and attentive.

"We're sorcerers…gods to you…with power you couldn't possibly understand."

"But you're evil."

Slater flashed another nefarious grin.

"Your deal with the Masters is the only reason you and your friend survived. Does that make you evil?"

Evelyn swallowed hard, because her previous sacrifice to the Masters had been the thing that saved them. Deep down, she feared surrendering again might be the only way to survive this fight. *But Adrian would never stand for it*, she thought to herself.

"I won't help you," Evelyn said, trying to remain strong.

"No… I believe you will…. I can feel them…. Their energy is strong around you…they are my family…my kin…and tonight, they will be free," Slater said, tracing the emblem on his ring with his other hand.

"No," she replied firmly.

Slater's demeanor shifted abruptly; the grin and playful air vanished, replaced by a surge of rage that seemed to ripple through him. For a moment, his features contorted, mirroring the crude, grotesque appearance of the giants from Evelyn's visions. She stared at him, glimpsing the monstrous essence tearing across his face. He met her gaze with a scowl and, in a burst of violence, struck her hard across the face.

"You will help me, or I'll kill you both."

Before Evelyn could react, Slater clamped his hand over the top of her head, his grip tightening like a vise. As he squeezed, Evelyn's shriek echoed through the room.

"I remember killing you before… I crushed your skull just like this," he hissed.

Screaming from the excruciating pain, blood began to drip from Evelyn's nostrils. Suddenly, Slater released his grip.

"Let's leave her here for a couple of hours to think about what I said," Slater said to Saul and Cavil.

They exited, leaving her alone in the dilapidated apartment. Alone, Evelyn sat in the sparse room, grappling with Slater's ominous words and the bleak reality of her situation. *Am I going to die tonight?* she wondered. Her thoughts turned to Adrian, who she knew was likely on his way to rescue her. Yet, if his plan failed, they would both be dead. In her desperation, she found herself wavering, considering Slater's offer as a means to survive, despite the shame and dread it stirred within her.

Wrestling with her thoughts, Evelyn watched as daylight slowly faded through the window, the sun dipping below the horizon beyond her view. Darkness was nearly complete when the sound of approaching footsteps disrupted the silence. Slater and his group returned, their presence heavy and silent in the room. Cavil wasted no time; he quickly untied her from the chair, pulled her to her feet, and ushered her out of the building to the van waiting ominously outside.

The van sped off, but it was only a short ride before it halted abruptly, and Evelyn knew instantly they were at the factory. They exited the van in front of the construction fence that separated the remnants of the Dyeworks tannery from the street. Under the glow of a nearby streetlamp stood Stewart, his glasses reflecting the harsh light of the van's headlights.

With Cavil holding Evelyn's arm tightly, they approached the fence where Stewart was waiting.

"Why is she here?" Stewart blurted out.

"Shut up," Saul snapped.

Evelyn couldn't take her eyes off Slater, haunted by the revelation of his true nature—the giant who had ended their lives in a past incarnation. Slater, noticing her fixated stare and sensing her fear, stepped closer.

"The only way to have the life you want, for yourself and your tall friend, is to do what I say."

Evelyn stood motionless. The temptation to strike a deal with them whispered promises of escape for her and Adrian, a chance to avoid a grim fate. But she knew in her heart that aligning with them was wrong, even if they offered an escape from certain death.

"Don't underestimate her," Stewart said, continuing to direct his words at Saul, who stood watching, amused. "I told you—her and her friend are dangerous."

Ignoring Stewart, Saul and Slater proceeded along the property line until they reached a gap in the fence. They slipped through, with Cavil pushing Evelyn ahead of him and Stewart following closely behind. The group navigated through the desolate site, stepping over scattered debris, chunks of concrete, and twisted metal. They made their way to one of the few walls still standing, which provided some concealment from the street view, further enhanced by the shadow of the construction fence.

Stopping on the other side of the wall, Evelyn's unease grew because despite being out in the open, they were alone.

Stewart looked around, clearly worried as well. "Are you going to tell me now why I'm here? I already told you there's nothing more I can do."

Cavil grabbed Stewart by the collar and forced him down to his knees. At that moment, Saul came forward, reached into his jacket and pulled out Ursula's knife, with a jagged blade and handle made of bone. He extended it towards Evelyn to take.

Evelyn's hand moved on its own, reaching out to take the knife. She couldn't stop herself, even though her hand shook with fear as she grasped the handle.

"You know what needs to be done," Saul whispered to her. "You've done it before."

Evelyn knew there was no turning back now.

"What are you doing?" Stewart whimpered, looking over to Saul.

"Don't look at me!" Saul barked. "She's the one with the knife."

Stewart looked up at Evelyn, hoping to find a hint of the friendly real estate agent he had known. But looking down at him, even as pathetic as he was, trembling before her, Evelyn struggled to feel any compassion. Slater watched with obvious amusement.

"Evelyn, please. I want nothing to do with this. Please, just let me go," Stewart pleaded.

In the distance, over the construction fence and across the street, Evelyn noticed a group of homeless individuals emerging from the alleys between buildings, clothes ragged and worn.

Suddenly, one of them—a rough-looking man with a disheveled beard—spotted their group. He quickly gestured to his companions, and in an instant, they scattered, vanishing into the darkness. *No witnesses,* she thought to herself. Slater stepped toward Evelyn, sensing her weakness. The moonlight cast harsh shadows on his face, accentuating the grey in his hair and the deep lines under his eyes.

"It's time," Slater commanded. "Do it, Evelyn. If you carry this out, I won't have to kill you again."

"What would Adrian say?" Stewart said, tears in his eyes.

God forgive me. Evelyn looked Stewart right in the eyes and then thrust the knife deep into his heart.

Stewart's anguished wail shattered the stillness as he collapsed, his body crumpling onto the ground. Blood seeped out beneath him, staining the earth. Evelyn shivered as she sensed the Masters' presence nearby.

Evelyn stood still, her hand holding the blood-stained knife. Her breaths came in rapid gasps, and her heart beat wildly in her chest. She couldn't tear her eyes away from Stewart's lifeless bloody body on the ground. The consequences of her actions frightened her now, aware that she had crossed a line with no chance of turning back.

Slater put his hand on Evelyn's head, gently petting her like a pet.

"Well done."

***

Adrian and Casey cautiously stepped out from under the safety of the trees near Echo Lake, making their way towards where they had parked by the side of the road. The town streets were eerily quiet as they passed through, and signs of recent turmoil caused by Ursula became more apparent once they reached Main Street, where deserted vehicles and shattered storefronts signaled the edge of the industrial district.

As they drew near the site of the collapsed Dyeworks factory, Adrian directed Casey to park the car down the street, about 50 yards away, to avoid detection. Once parked, Adrian opened his duffle bag and slipped on the brass knuckles, then reached back into the bag and gripped the steel pipe, ready for what might come next.

"Make sure you keep your distance from what's about to happen. It's not going to be safe here."

Casey reached out, and put her hand on his, feeling the tenseness of his grip on the pipe.

"Be careful. You don't have to die. I'll be waiting here," she said, tears beginning to well in her eyes.

Adrian nodded in a somber manner, his expression betraying his feelings of remorse. He then opened the car door and got out, pausing to stare down the street where the rundown Dyeworks factory stood, its decaying form barely visible behind the construction barriers. A deep feeling resonated within him, that Evelyn was there. Adrian slowly made his way forward, crouching behind parked cars and using bushes as cover. He carefully moved closer and closer until he reached the gap in the construction fence that he had created earlier.

Peering through the gap at the ruins, where only a few walls still stood, Adrian could make out shadows shifting within. He moved closer, weaving through slabs of concrete and mounds of bricks, until he found a strategic vantage point. From here, he could clearly see Saul, Cavil, and Slater gathered on the other side of a crumbling wall, surrounded by piles of rubble and twisted rebar. In the center, Evelyn stood facing them, her expression vacant. In her hands, she held Ursula's knife, and it was stained with blood.

Adrian struggled to comprehend what was happening until he saw Stewart's lifeless body lying on the ground. He abandoned his initial plan of sneaking up on them when he realized she had willingly joined in their dark ritual to summon the Masters. The sound of crunching debris and shattered glass under his boots filled the air as he approached them. Saul noticed Adrian's approach and greeted him with a smile.

"Look who we have here," he said, alerting the others.

All eyes shifted to Adrian, but his focus remained solely on Evelyn. When she finally turned to look at him, their eyes met, and he saw a profound change within her.

"Evelyn, are you okay?"

"I'm fine." Her voice was cold and flat.

"Remember who you are, what we've stood for," he said, stepping closer. "Their darkness is not power—it's a curse."

Evelyn looked away, her face revealing the struggle within.

"Adrian, we don't have to die like we did before. We can live together in this life. Don't you want that?"

Adrian clenched his left hand, the brass knuckles pressing against his skin. His right hand tightened its grip on the steel pipe. "I'm not afraid of dying."

"Useless," Slater hissed, showing his disdain.

Saul signaled Cavil, ready for this fight. He moved towards Adrian and stopped about ten feet away, then pulled a pistol from under his shirt, aiming it straight at Adrian's heart.

"No, please don't do this!" Evelyn cried out.

Adrian launched the metal pipe at Cavil to disarm him before he could pull the trigger. The pipe twisted through the air and struck Cavil's hand, causing him to drop his gun. Before he could reach for it, Adrian sprinted towards him and slammed into him, sending them both tumbling to the ground. Adrian rained down punches on him, with the brass knuckles aimed at his sides, hoping to shatter his ribs.

Cavil reeled from the pain but still managed to push him away and stagger to his feet. With rapid steps, Adrian closed the distance, ducking under Cavil's extended arms to deliver more powerful blows to his midsection. Each punch landed with a sickening crunch. Blood started to trickle from the corner of Cavil's mouth as he gasped for air, his breaths ragged and desperate. Trying to retreat, his path was blocked by two large concrete slabs.

Cornered, he attempted to defend himself, but Adrian's blows kept coming, each one more vicious and brutal than the last. Cavil's face began to deform under the relentless assault, his features twisting in agony. Finally, he crumpled to the ground, battered and bloodied.

Adrian stood over Cavil's motionless body, breathing heavily, his heart beating through his chest. *He's dead.* He looked up to see Saul and Slater staring at him with hate in their eyes. Evelyn remained expressionless toward violence she had just witnessed.

"We can end this, Adrian. They're going to kill you…and then me. Please. Let's have one life together."

Adrian, weary to his bones, felt the allure of her words—a chance at peace, rest from the endless fight. Yet, he knew it wasn't an option.

"You've taken one of ours. Perhaps it's time we return the favor," Saul said, gesturing towards someone behind Adrian.

Adrian's heart sank as he turned around and saw what he'd wanted to avoid come true. Casey, overwhelmed with concern for Evelyn, had abandoned her hiding spot and was now standing out in the open at the edge of the site.

"Stay away!" he shouted.

Evelyn glanced back at her friend and stared with emotionless, unrecognizable eyes. Slater moved towards Casey, anticipating their encounter. As he neared Adrian, he whispered something in a low tone, just loud enough for him to hear.

"I remember killing you and your wife."

The words struck Adrian, a harsh reminder of their past—the joy they once shared, only to lose again. As he gazed at Slater's face, a fleeting distortion passed over it, revealing hints of the monstrous giant he used to be.

Adrian lashed out with brass knuckles, aiming to crush Slater's skull. But Slater swiftly caught Adrian's fist in one hand, then yanked it so violently that Adrian's shoulder dislocated. A sharp cry of pain escaped him, instinctively clutching at his injured shoulder with his other hand. Slater then advanced, his fingers closing tightly around Adrian's throat.

"Come here," Slater screamed at Evelyn.

She moved forward and Saul followed closely behind.

"I've already closed the portal at Echo Lake," Adrian croaked. "All that remains is for me to die…"

Slater's eyes widened with a mix of anger and disbelief. Muttering curses under his breath, he delivered a sharp blow to Adrian's temple and hurled him to the ground. Adrian hit the pavement hard and didn't get up.

"Then let's do what needs to be done… Evelyn," he commanded, "give me the knife."

Evelyn stepped forward, handing the knife to Slater. He smeared Stewart's blood across his tongue in a ritualistic gesture and then tossed the knife aside. With his palms upturned to the sky, Slater closed his eyes. Out of nowhere, the sky above started to shimmer with brilliant lights, creating a surreal spectacle. Evelyn heard the eerie whispers of spirits in her ear, their voices sending chills down her spine. Shadows moved around her, twisted figures that darted back and forth, barely visible. Casey moved closer, her eyes locked on Evelyn, trying to penetrate the thick veil of malevolent energy enveloping them.

They were surrounded by the screeches of dark creatures, the same chilling sounds that had echoed through the tunnels under

Dyeworks. The horrifying noises stirred Adrian from his unconscious state. As he saw Cavil's motionless body lying a few feet away, he mustered the strength to get to his feet, despite his own injuries and the daunting task of facing Slater alone.

To give Adrian a moment to recover, Casey walked over to Slater with a calm demeanor.

"If she's part of this, then I am too," she stated firmly, stepping closer to him.

Slater opened his eyes and looked at her with disdain. "I have no use for you..."

Adrian summoned all his remaining strength and reached for a jagged piece of rebar protruding from the cracked concrete. He sprang up and charged towards Slater, holding the rebar like a baseball bat. Swinging with all his might, the rebar collided with Slater's skull, producing a sickening sound, splattering blood all over Casey, who stood nearby. Slater's head separated from his body, thudding onto the ground and rolling a few feet. Blood gushed from the decapitated body as it slowly toppled over. The screeches that had been echoing from beneath the ground went silent.

"What have you done?" Saul barked, beginning to cough violently.

"It's finished," Adrian said, catching his breath.

He turned towards Evelyn, hoping to see a glimpse of relief in her eyes, but there was none.

"We can leave now..."

"It's too late," Evelyn replied.

Wiping blood from his mouth with his handkerchief, Saul's eyes darted to the ground and caught sight of Cavil's gun at his feet. He lunged for the weapon, then stood up, and aimed it directly at Adrian. He fired three shots. Adrian stood still, heart pounding, as the bullets seemed to whiz past him. Then, from behind, he heard a strangled gasp. Turning his head sharply, his eyes widened in horror. Evelyn, standing just a few feet away, was clutching her chest where the bullets had struck. Her eyes were filled with shock and pain as she fell backwards, collapsing into a heap of rubble on the ground. Saul aimed the gun again, but it jammed.

"Fuck," he muttered, tapping it with his other hand in frustration. Seizing the moment, Adrian sprinted forward and tackled Saul to the ground, crashing hard into a pile of rubble strewn with sharp pieces of rebar. He felt Saul's body suddenly go limp beneath him.

Breathing hard, Adrian slowly stood up. At his feet, Saul let out an anguished moan. Adrian looked down and saw a sharp piece of rebar poking through Saul's side, blood streaming from his mouth. The jagged metal protruded grotesquely, tearing through fabric and flesh. Dark, viscous blood pooled around the wound, spreading quickly. Saul's eyes, wide with pain and fear, stared up at Adrian, his mouth moving soundlessly as he struggled for breath. Then he let out one last dying gasp.

Reeling from the shock, Casey began wiping Slater's blood from her face, unable to move her feet. Adrian quickly ran to Evelyn's side and knelt next to her.

"I'm here; we're going to be okay," he said, holding her in his arms.

"I'm so…sorry. This is…all…my fault," Evelyn sobbed.

"No, that's not true," Adrian said firmly. He then turned to Casey. 'Call an ambulance!" he shouted.

Casey, trembling, fumbled for her phone. She moved slowly towards them, her face pale with fear, dreading the sight of Evelyn in her dire state.

"Am I…gonna…die?"

"No," he said, lacking conviction in his tone.

Adrian looked down at Evelyn and could see both bullet wounds, one in her chest and the other in her stomach. He placed his hands over them, trying to stop the bleeding, but the blood just oozed through his fingers. Choking back his own tears, he tried to distract her.

"We won. They're all gone."

Evelyn forced a weak smile, then furrowed her brow in confusion, "You're hurt too."

Adrian saw the blood seeping through his shirt. He pulled it up, revealing the bullet hole.

"I love you," Evelyn said, her eyes fluttering.

In that moment, he knew they both wouldn't make it, but in dying, the portals would not be opened again. He pulled Evelyn closer. "I love you," he whispered. "Now we can be together forever."

She reached out, her hand trembling, and he took it in his own, squeezing gently. He leaned in, his lips meeting hers softly for a fleeting kiss. When her grip slackened in his hand, she let out one final, shuddering breath, and he knew she was gone. Adrian slowly laid his body down next to hers, his arm draped over her, then closed his eyes. His chest heaved, and the life left his body—both of them passing into the next world together.

Casey let out a scream of anguish that echoed across the desolate landscape. Overwhelmed by grief, she fell to her knees, sobbing uncontrollably, unable to look at their bodies.

Just then, the silence was shattered by the piercing wail of police sirens. Blue and red lights flashed down the street, as a convoy of police cars rushed toward Dyeworks. Officers exited their vehicles and sprinted toward the construction fencing, quickly locating the opening. Following closely behind, the mayor stepped out of the back of a police cruiser and hurried to catch up with the officers as they moved through the gap onto the site.

What they saw was grim. The bodies of Slater, Cavil, and Saul were sprawled lifeless on the ground, while nearby, the two lovers lay intertwined in death.

The mayor approached Casey, gesturing for the officers to lower their weapons and continue scanning the area.

"You're safe now…"

Casey managed a silent nod.

"They saved us, didn't they?"

"Yes."

He offered his hand to her. "I'll take care of this. No one will know you were here."

CHAPTER 14

AFTER THE LOSS of her best friend, Casey took on the responsibility of organizing the funerals for both Evelyn and Adrian. In the immediate aftermath of their passing, she poured all of her energy into ensuring they received proper goodbyes. As the sole heir named in Evelyn's will, Casey found herself responsible for organizing her best friend's funeral and managing the possessions she left behind. It was a bittersweet task for Casey, but it allowed her to honor Evelyn's memory during one of the most difficult moments in her life.

As Casey handled Evelyn's affairs following her passing, she discovered the commitment Evelyn had made to rent the upstairs apartment to Mrs. Sanderson, a kind elderly woman. With the help of Trevor and Cam from Evelyn's office, Casey gathered all necessary details and promptly arranged for Mrs. Sanderson to receive the lease, honoring Evelyn's promise. Regarding the downstairs apartment, Casey chose to delay any decisions until after the funeral, giving herself time to consider what to do with it. Any surplus funds from Evelyn's estate were directed towards charitable donations. Additionally, Casey allocated a portion of the monthly rent that Evelyn would have received to support the local homeless shelter near the old Dyeworks factory.

During this difficult period, Mayor Jenkins stood by Casey and offered his support. Together, they devised a plan to keep the details of the recent incidents in Baneford under wraps, protected from public scrutiny and media exposure. Interestingly, at the same time, the buzz surrounding the archaeological site at Echo Lake began to fade as media coverage subsided. The initial international interest in the discovery also waned, with skeptics emerging to question the bones' authenticity and the accuracy of the carbon dating results.

On the day of the funeral, a large contingent of the community gathered at the town cemetery to pay their respects to Evelyn and, by extension, Adrian. There was a gentleness in the air, now accentuated by the crispness of spring. Two new gravestones had been placed side by side, purchased by Casey as a loving tribute to her dear friends, and adorned with fresh flowers.

Casey looked out at the crowd, observing the multitude of faces. She had learned Adrian's last name only in preparation for this day. Surrounding her were individuals from her hometown who had known Evelyn since childhood, and many Casey didn't recognize.

Mayor Jenkins stepped forward to address the assembly of mourners first. He surveyed the crowd, taking a moment to compose himself before he began.

"I had the privilege of knowing Evelyn and Adrian. They were remarkable individuals, deeply committed to the welfare of our community." He paused, his eyes briefly lingering on the gravestones. "Today, as we come together to honor their memory, and their impact, which in many ways, will always remain beyond words."

Once Mayor Jenkins had finished his speech, he made his way over to Evelyn's grave. With great care, he laid his mayoral pin on top of the tombstone as a final tribute and farewell from the town. As he turned to leave, a soft breeze rustled through the trees. It was then Casey's turn to take the podium.

"Evelyn was my best friend, my sister, and a beloved member of our community. Even in her toughest times, she was kind and loyal. None of you knew Adrian. He wasn't from here, but he was her guardian, and a guardian of this town. He was brave." Casey paused to wipe tears from her eyes. "Evil exists in our world. In the fight against darkness, Evelyn and Adrian stood their ground. Even though they're gone now, I know their spirits will live on." Her voice trembled, as she stepped away from the podium, tears streaming down her face.

As the ceremony neared its conclusion, a small jazz band positioned near the edge of the cemetery began their performance. The first somber notes of a saxophone filled the air, its deep, melancholic tones weaving gracefully through the crowd. The music prompted tears to glisten in the eyes of the mourners. When the final note drifted off into the quiet of the afternoon, the assembled began to slowly disperse.

That evening, as the sun set, its golden rays enveloped their graves in a warm, serene glow. Meanwhile, far across the Atlantic, Maruf stood beneath the vast night sky, his eyes fixed on the belt stars of Orion. A gentle sense of peace settled over him, comforted by the knowledge that his friends had found their freedom.

Casey was one of the last people to leave the cemetery. She thanked the priest and headed for her car. Exhausted, she had barely slept or eaten since she lost her best friend. But it was over now, and she knew she had to take care of herself. Evie would want her to. As Casey got closer, she noticed something on her SUV. It looked like someone had smeared mud on her windshield. "Really," Casey said out loud, "who vandalizes cars at a funeral?" Someone had drawn concentric circles on the window. When she arrived at the driver's side door, she saw that it wasn't mud, but blood. *This isn't over*, she realized.

ABOUT THE AUTHOR

ALI KADEN grew up between the US and Egypt, considering both countries "home." Adopting a broad view of the world, he's endlessly fascinated by the diversity of belief systems, mythologies, and cultures. Expectedly, Ali enjoys introducing multicultural elements into each of his stories. As an author, Ali hopes to bring stories to life that readers find deeply moving, creative, and fun. He believes good literature can save lives, or at the very least, make dark days brighter. Passionate about the craft, he loves to use potent descriptions, captivating metaphors, and varied plot structures in his writing. When he's not working on new stories, he co-manages a real estate business in Boston and spends time with his wife, young daughter, and their loyal terrier, Joyous. A fan of boxing, Ali can also often be found hitting the heavy bag to the *Rocky* soundtrack at his local gym.

CHECK OUT *KALI ON THE ROPES*, A STANDALONE ACTION-SUSPENSE NOVEL. VISIT ALIKADENBOOKS.COM TO GET THE LATEST UPDATES.

www.ingramcontent.com/pod-product-compliance
Lightning Source LLC
LaVergne TN
LVHW041706060526
838201LV00043B/604